CONSEQUENCES OF THEIR WEDDING CHARADE

CATHY WILLIAMS

MILLS & BOON

First published in Great Britain 2022
by Mills & Boon, an imprint of HarperCollins*Publishers* Ltd,
1 London Bridge Street, London, SE1 9GF

www.harpercollins.co.uk

HarperCollins*Publishers*
1st Floor, Watermarque Building,
Ringsend Road, Dublin 4, Ireland

Large Print edition 2022

Consequences of Their Wedding Charade © 2022 Cathy Williams

ISBN: 978-0-263-29529-0

06/22

MIX
Paper from
responsible sources
FSC
www.fsc.org   FSC™ C007454

CHAPTER ONE

'FLOWERS? FOR ME? An hour and a half ahead of schedule, Curtis, and you've come bearing flowers…heather…narcissi…pussy willow, no less! I had no idea you were so well acquainted with the English winter garden!'

From his towering height of six foot three, Curtis Hamilton looked down on his much more diminutive godfather and grinned.

'I know absolutely nothing about English winter gardens,' he drawled, shutting the front door on a snowy February landscape and taking a few seconds to breathe in the familiarity of his godfather's cottage, with its unique smells of a house lived in by a bookish bachelor with a flair for home cooking. 'Nor,' he continued with lazy amusement, as he divested himself of his cashmere coat and handmade Italian loafers, both of which were ridiculously unsuitable for heavy snow in Cambridgeshire but there hadn't been a flake when he'd left

London, 'do I know a thing about flowers of any description, English or otherwise. Got Julia, my PA, to get them for me. And, just for the record, the flowers aren't for you, William.'

'No, I suspected not. Care to divulge, dear boy?'

'In due course. What can I smell?' He sniffed the air but his eyes were trained on his godfather, looking for anything that might hint that things weren't as they should be. From the very moment he had walked through the doors of the foster care home where Curtis had been miserably languishing—an eight-year-old statistic in an uncaring and impersonal machine—he had bought himself all the love and affection Curtis had within him to give.

After his health scare eighteen months previously, William Farrow had retreated into himself, knocked back by a body that had let him down combined with his scheduled retirement from the University of Cambridge, where he had lectured in Classics for decades.

A double whammy.

But, thankfully, right now he looked himself, bustling ahead of Curtis towards the kitchen with the flowers, giving a detailed account of what was on the menu for dinner, from where he'd bought the ingredients to how they had been put to use and leaving nothing out in the telling.

He was a small, round man who always dressed formally. Curtis often teased him that it was on the off-chance royalty might just pop by unannounced for a cup of tea.

Curtis knew that tonight his godfather would have made a special effort and was not surprised to see that he was wearing a snazzy red bow tie with his crisp blue shirt, and some *slacks*, as he insisted on calling them. Not quite funeral formal but definitely not the sort of casual gear most people might associate with dinner at a kitchen table.

Curtis's heart swelled with affection. In a life where emotions were never allowed to intrude, his godfather was the only person who could lay claim to his unconditional love. Neither ever spoke of it, but Curtis was very much aware of the fact that William had rescued him from his damaged past and saved him from the unknown horrors of a future that would not have been kind to a child raised by a drug addict and then thrown into foster care when his mother had finally overdosed. There were so many statistics in that setting—children who were lost for ever when they were spat out as young adults—and he could easily have become one of them.

'I haven't seen you for over three months. Yes, you managed Christmas Day here, but that was the sum of it.' William busied himself with a vase but there was intent behind that throwaway observation and Curtis, sitting at the pine kitchen table, breathing in the fragrant aromas of beef and oyster pie, felt a prick of intense guilt.

'I know and I can only apologise for that. Would you believe me if I told you that I would have visited if I could have?'

'I would,' William said wryly, 'which is the problem. You work too hard, Curtis.' He stood back to inspect his handiwork with the flowers and then carefully placed the vase on the dresser against the wall before bringing a couple of wine glasses to the table.

'It's a blessing and a curse,' Curtis murmured, mind wandering as the conversation took a familiar turn.

Where was she?

He'd shqwn up with the flowers which, admittedly, had been a tiny bit bruised because he'd chucked them on the passenger seat of his Range Rover and then inadvertently dumped his computer bag on top, but still perfectly acceptable as a prelude to a favour.

But where had she been? At six o'clock on a Thursday evening in the depths of winter? On the outskirts of Cambridge? With snow falling? Was there anything to actually *do* on the outskirts of Cambridge on a snowy winter's evening? When he thought about that, his mind hit a road block.

At any rate, she hadn't been in and he'd been so surprised that he'd waited an inordinately long time in the freezing weather before giving up on the doorbell and making his way over to his godfather, who lived twenty minutes away.

He surfaced to the tail-end of his godfather warning him about blood pressure, stress and all the various ailments that could afflict someone who worked too much.

And thereafter followed a comfortable journey for both of them. Gentle nagging, curiosity about some of the bigger projects Curtis was working on—state-of-the-art buildings that defied laws of gravity, the vast commercial sites which were additions to his multimillion-pound portfolio—and then, over the beef pie and roast potatoes, the inevitable questioning about the future.

A wife…children…all those things which had eluded William Farrow, making it doubly important for his godson to achieve, apparently.

How could anyone know what might be good for someone if they'd never experienced it themselves? His godfather had never been married, had never had children, had never, to Curtis's knowledge, desired either.

So where was the logic in recommending those very things to him? Certainly, when it came to lessons learned on the journey through life, his were resoundingly clear when it came to love and all the happy-ever-afters it always seemed to preface.

Not for him.

He was no longer a lost child, pouring love into a parent who had no time for him. He knew better than to hand his heart over to anyone. Waiting by a window with no food to eat for a mother who had viewed parenting as something way down the list of priorities had put paid to all his illusions and if that hadn't been enough, then there had been the shambolic disaster with Caitlin...

He shut the door on that particular memory with a decisive clang.

The subject of a rosy future that wasn't on the cards for him was adroitly shelved when William asked without preamble, as they sipped coffee after an exemplary pie, 'So who, dear boy, were the flowers destined for?'

Which focused Curtis instantly on the thorny question he had been asking himself for the past couple of hours.

'Jessica, as it happens. Rang her doorbell for half an hour! No answer. Where the heck is the woman?'

'Flowers...for *Jess*?'

Curtis flushed, glanced at his watch and fidgeted in the chair, which suddenly felt constricting. His godfather's sharp blue eyes were pinned to his face with undisguised curiosity.

'*Why?*'

'It's not a crime to buy a bunch of flowers

for someone,' Curtis said with just a hint of defensiveness in his voice.

How was it that in the world of the billionaire he was the leader of the pack and yet in a cottage on the outskirts of Ely he was reduced to perspiring round the collar at the prospect of a couple of awkward questions from his sixty-eight-year-old godfather?

When he had absolutely nothing to hide whatsoever.

'I…er…it's been a while since I saw her. Naturally, I've emailed a couple of times… always good to know what's…er…happening around here…'

'You mean you get in touch when you want to find out if I'm all right…' William said shrewdly. 'Make sure the old codger hasn't fallen into a state of utter despair because his ticker isn't what it used to be…' He chortled and waved an admonishing finger. 'Appreciate the concern, my son, but I'm doing fine! And now that you ask about Jess,' he continued smugly, 'the girl's finally doing what I've been advising her to do for the past two years. She's getting out there and dating!' He cast a jaundiced eye over the flowers. 'And no suitor worth his salt is going to appreciate some other chap bringing flowers to his intended!'

Curtis had never heard such a string of old-fashioned terms in his life before. *Suitor? Chap? Intended?* Never mind that he was *none* of those things!

'In that case—' he flattened his hands on the table and rose with fluid grace to his feet '—I'll take doughnuts…'

Jess surfaced groggily to the insistent ringing of her doorbell.

When she looked at her phone, it was to discover that it was a little after eight. That made it an hour past her usual waking up time, whether she was working or not.

Thank God it was half-term and she was *not* because she would have had a crazy rush to get to the school in time.

Nevertheless, she felt slothful at having slept in, even though it had been a long and wearisome night.

How could a date with a friend of a friend of a friend, who had sounded so perfect on paper, have turned out to be so…dull?

He was a fellow teacher at a school in York,

he had a degree in philosophy from Oxford Uni, which should have guaranteed an active and energetic mind, plus he taught PE, so how bad could it be, and yet...

She shook her head, flung on the dressing gown from behind the bedroom door and flew to the front door.

She lived in a tiny terraced house and whenever the postman decided to do what he did best—relax on the doorbell for minutes on end—she was terrified that one of her lovely but extremely old neighbours would be upset at the resulting din.

She pulled open the front door to yet another grim and wintry sky and was busily tying the cord of her dressing gown tightly round her as her mouth fell open when for a few seconds she had the sort of brain fog that only descended when one of her kids at school got it into their head that paying attention in class meant talking at full volume over what she was trying to say.

Curtis.

Curtis Hamilton...six foot plus of prime alpha male, so insanely sexy that perfectly normal human beings with their heads firmly screwed on started doing stupid things when he decided to turn the full wattage of his attention on them.

Jess had known him for so long, had been his *friend* for such a long time, that she should have been immune to his looks, his charm and his wit but she never had been.

He'd been ten and she was three years younger when he had appeared at their primary school and, of course, all focus had been on the new kid.

She'd seen him around and about but it was when her mum had taken the job as housekeeper to his godfather that she had really become friends with him. She could remember long summer holidays, poling over to the Farrow place, as her mother used to call it, hanging around while her mum cleaned and tidied and sometimes sat and had a cup of tea with Mr Farrow, an adorable little man with fastidious ways and a knack when it came to baking.

Curtis was older but he was patient. He'd never seemed to mind taking her fishing or including her with his group of friends. Looking back, she could see that he had sensed her insecurities, her inherent shyness, the bookish personality that had concealed, as she had entered adolescence, her intense awkwardness at being the 'big girl' in the class.

Later, she thought that maybe he *had* minded, but had been too kind to say anything.

As they'd got older there'd been a brief spell when he seemed to disappear but then, when she turned thirteen, she suddenly seemed to become *visible*. He'd told her about his plans to make it big, laughed when she quizzed him about his girlfriends, rolled his eyes and confided that he just didn't have sticking power when it came to relationships...

She preciously guarded that place in his life. Girlfriends came and went but she was always there and how dependent she had gradually become on the confidence he gave her, patching up her anxious hesitation about her looks, making her feel good about herself at a time in her teenage years when being 'one of the lads' had not been what she'd wanted. Her parents had always been there for her, but they were biased. She'd needed a different kind of affirmation and he'd given it to her in spades just by being there for her.

And what would she had done if he hadn't

been there for her when her beloved dad had died five years previously? Curtis had been away but had returned as soon as he'd heard and he'd been the perfect shoulder to cry on.

Childish adoration and teenage infatuation usually never stayed the same, fizzling out as Life took over, but not for her. For her, those feelings had deepened into something else.

How she'd wished that he could have been more than just her buddy, but by then she'd fully read and understood the writing on the wall. The category she occupied was unique but it would never extend where she wanted it.

It frightened her to think just how long she would have stayed there, happy with crumbs, in defiance of all the signposts that had been emblazoned for her to follow from the beginning...if he hadn't got engaged to Caitlin Smyth.

That was a year and a half ago and the engagement had been short-lived because Caitlin had broken it off, but it had been the learning curve Jess had badly needed to turn away from the spell he had always weaved over her.

She had purposely avoided him for the past few months. She'd answered emails and occasionally spoken to him on the phone when he'd called, but she'd made sure to be busy every time she knew he'd be turning up to visit William.

School trip...visiting her mum, who had moved to Devon to be closer to her sister... buried under work so, oops, so sorry but no way could she snatch any time off...

The list had been exhaustive, but she'd succeeded. On the rare occasion when she had been in his presence she'd made sure to time it so that other people were around, a safety buffer against herself and her weakness.

Until now.

Because here he was, at her front door, with a box in his hand and a smile on his face and looking every bit as wickedly sexy as he had the last time she'd set eyes on him.

Of course the unbuttoned cashmere coat was crazy in this weather, as were the loafers. Underneath, she could see he was in a pair of faded jeans and his old rugby jumper.

So beautiful, so sinfully perfect in every way... Thick brown hair streaked with caramel, green eyes the colour of the sea in a certain light, the hint of a dimple in his chin and thick, dark lashes to die for.

'Are you going to let me in or should I start calling the paramedics to come out because I'm about to get hypothermia?'

'Curtis!'

'Ah, so you do remember who I am... Move aside, Jess, I need to get out of this cold. My coat and my shoes weren't made for snow.' He nudged past her as she fell back and helplessly watched him dump the box on the little table against the wall so that he could get rid of the coat. 'Don't tell me, it was crazy to come up here with nothing but a wool coat, but who knew that it would be snowing? Thought I'd left that old waterproof in the shed but it would seem not.'

He looked at her and she fought down a blush.

She'd woken from her slumber when he'd got engaged, recognised where she stood, acknowledged where she'd *never* stand, and she'd accordingly made a concerted effort to get her house in order.

So she was never going to be the sort of petite, adorable little blonde thing he was attracted to. She was five ten and had always been prone to generous curves. When her dad had died, her curves had unfortunately expanded with her comfort eating, but bit by bit she had cut back on the chocolate and in the past few months had returned to her usual figure.

'Where are your specs?' he asked, frowning and strolling towards her, green eyes intent on her face, scrutinising as though she had somehow contrived to let him down by withholding vital information about her eyesight.

'Laser surgery,' she said, gathering her scattered self-control and preceding him into the kitchen, where she waited until he was seated at her kitchen table before asking him what he was doing here.

'Doughnuts.' He nodded briefly to the box that he had deposited on the kitchen counter. 'Since when were you interested in having laser surgery?'

'You came here to bring me…*doughnuts*?'

'Why not?' He shrugged. 'What else are friends for?'

'Curtis, I was asleep when you rang the doorbell.'

'You do look a bit groggy. Late night?' His eyebrows shot up and he shot her a wolfish grin. 'Don't answer that. At least, not yet.'

'I need to get dressed.'

'You've done something to your hair as well...'

'Curtis, I'll be back in a sec, but honestly... today's a very busy day for me...'

'Doing what? It's half-term. William told me. So you can't possibly be going to the school.'

'Teachers don't just work during term time and there's a lot going on at the moment,' she gritted, and he grinned and patted the chair next to him.

'No need for you to change. I'm accustomed to seeing you *ébouriffé*...'

Jess ignored him. Yes, he had seen her dishevelled a million times in the past, notably one night when she was eighteen and he'd been back from university, having broken up with yet another small blonde called Mickey. He had turned up at her mother's house and they had watched two horror movies in a row, making their way through several bags of crisps and a bottle of wine. By then the childish adoration and the teenage infatuation had coalesced into something altogether more dangerous.

She changed fast. Suddenly self-conscious about her new and improved figure, she donned some old sweats and an extremely baggy jumper. She would have tied her hair back but he was right, she'd changed her hair along with everything else.

Instead of long and utterly unruly, it was now shoulder-length and more or less manageable. Tying it back was no longer an option.

She paused, looked at herself in the mirror. Still way too tall but the shorter hair suited her, framed her face, and it was nice not wearing specs. Her eyes were an unusual shade of deep, navy blue. No specs made the most of them.

She took a deep breath and returned to the kitchen to find him halfway through one of the doughnuts, having pushed back his chair so that he could stretch his long legs out at an angle.

'Aren't you going to have a doughnut?' He nodded to the box and she shook her head.

'Maybe later.'

He'd kicked off the loafers and she tried not

to stare at his feet as she moved to make them coffee.

Her nervous system was all over the place and she hated the fact that he could show up here and after all this time, after all her strenuous efforts to move on from limbo land, could *still* manage to have such a dramatic effect on her.

It was as though his larger than life presence had sucked the oxygen out of the air, leaving it difficult for her to breathe and she was so acutely conscious of his eyes on her as she stirred the boiling water into the coffee. Her entire body felt weird and prickly.

Before, she had been aware of him. Before, he had got under her skin, made her blush, sent her thoughts into disarray. But now that she had decided that he was forbidden fruit he was having an even more devastating effect on her senses and she knew that she had to control her reactions. He wasn't going to be around for long. She would urge him out just as soon as he'd finished his cup of coffee and then she would perhaps think about going to see her mum.

Or maybe not. Would that be a little too close to running away?

Certainly she would be letting his godfather down because she had promised to do two days with William working on his memoirs. It was a labour of love he had begun when he'd retired from lecturing and she helped transcribe them once a week, using it as an opportunity to have a chat and some dinner with him, make sure he was okay because she knew he was lonely at times.

'So…have you been avoiding me, Jessica Carr?' Curtis sipped his coffee, looked at her over the rim of the mug, his green eyes amused and questioning.

'Don't be crazy. Why would I avoid you, Curtis?'

'No idea, but I'm open to suggestions…'

'I've been busy. There's been a lot of fundraising at the school to help pay for the new wing and computer equipment. I've had a lot on my plate.'

'I know. Seems there's been a lot on your plate every time I've tried to arrange to see you when I've been here… You know what they say about all work and no play. But no…

wait… I hear through the grapevine that life hasn't been a case of all work for you of late…'

'What are you talking about?'

'Dropped by yesterday evening on the way to William but you weren't in. Hot date, I gather?' He grinned, his keen green eyes pinned to her face.

'You're so nosy.' She looked at him impatiently but the weight of history between them… How could she not respond to the teasing in his voice? She smiled and rolled her eyes. 'You *do* know that my private life is none of your business, Curtis.'

'If it's not my business, then whose is it? So? How did it go? Where did you meet him?'

'A friend of a friend and yes, thank you, it went very well. He's a teacher, like me, so we have a lot in common.'

'Sounds dull. Don't they say that opposites attract?'

'How do you find your godfather?' She changed the subject before she could become immersed in a conversation instinct told her to avoid. 'He seemed a little subdued when I saw him a week ago.'

'Subdued? How? He's always upbeat when I talk to him on the phone.'

'He doesn't want to worry you, Curtis.'

'Why would he think that he would worry me by being honest about anything that might be bothering him?' There was impatience and bemusement in his voice.

'Why do you think?'

He frowned and tilted his head to one side. 'Am I sensing an atmosphere between us?'

Jess felt the charm within that utterly sexy drawl feather over her and she had to fight not to shiver with treacherous awareness because this was what he was so good at…this was what made Curtis Hamilton such a health hazard when it came to the opposite sex. It wasn't just about those incredible looks or the money, what was *really* dangerous about him was the fact that he was so gifted at interacting. He knew how to listen, he picked up on things quickly, knew how to steer a conversation to elicit those little confidences you might not have wanted to impart. The very fact that they had been friends for so long, on such familiar terms, made her all the more conscious of the dangers of being lured back to that place from which she knew she had to flee. She had fallen for a guy who only saw her as a one-dimensional girl next door.

She had no intention of admitting to any kind of *atmosphere* between them, but she was certainly going to tell him what she thought on the matter of his godfather, of whom she was deeply fond.

'He's in awe of you, Curtis.' This was the most blunt she could remember being, but then it was also the first time he had been away for such a long period of time—several weeks, only popping back for Christmas. Into that void, Jess had certainly noticed signs of depression, something she was well adept at spotting given her own mother's descent into mild depression following her husband's death.

'Don't be ridiculous.'

'Sometimes you can be so…*blind*. Honestly!' She clicked her tongue as he continued to frown, mulling over what she had said. 'He doesn't want to bother you, Curtis. You're his golden godson who's conquered the world… You're his pride and joy who got a first in

Maths at Cambridge and then developed an app to deal with weight load that had every architect and engineering company in the world begging to pay you a king's ransom for it. You're the whiz-kid who was already formulating a property portfolio at twenty-three whilst opening his own company to deal with sexy, high-end constructions and then, as if that weren't enough, began taking over companies and making yet more millions...'

'Stop, please.' He held up his hands in a gesture of mock surrender. 'It's all going to go to my head and you wouldn't want that, would you?' His tone was light. His mind was whirring. William? Depressed? Just thinking about it sent a coil of clammy alarm curling through him. When it came to the rest of the world, and certainly when it came to women, he might have locked his heart away and thrown away the key to protect himself from ever being hurt, but not so when it came to his godfather.

'I think he feels that you might find it boring if he starts dwelling on his own problems. And these past few weeks... You haven't been around that much. I guess, when you have been here, he just wants to enjoy your company without bringing up anything troublesome...'

'Do you realise that you're the only woman who has ever been able to talk to me like this?' His voice was absent-minded, his thoughts dwelling on what she had said, his keen brain already trying to source ways to remedy a problem of which he had been unaware.

Jess looked at him, so familiar, so stupidly dear to her, so oblivious to how she felt about him.

He stretched and she compulsively and guiltily drank in the sinewy length of his body and the sliver of hard skin exposed as the jumper rode up ever so slightly.

She wondered whether he was seeing anyone. Many times, she got wind of girlfriends thanks to the diligent paparazzi, who couldn't seem to get enough of someone clever, stupidly rich and insanely good-looking. It was as though they'd hit jackpot with him and so kept bouncing back to cover whatever he happened to be up to. All had been quiet on the Western Front for some time.

Not your business! She shook her head, clearing it to focus on what he had said.

'You say that but that's because all those poor women you date are so desperate to be with you that they'd do anything to hang on, including agreeing with everything you say. If you ask me, it's not healthy...'

He burst out laughing and looked at her with warm appreciation. 'Thank God I have one nag in my life, making sure my ego doesn't over-inflate.'

'Thanks for the compliment, Curtis.' But something inside her twisted painfully even though she knew that actually, in his eyes, it really *was* a compliment.

'I'll keep an eye on him while I'm here and I've wrapped up a heck of a lot of pressing business abroad, so my time is going to be a little less pressured for the next few months. I'd planned,' he mused, 'on staying for the week-end but maybe I'll stretch it out a bit longer. Hang around for a week instead. What would we do without the World Wide Web? Business on the go wherever you happen to be and thankfully the internet connection at the cottage is first rate.' He sat up abruptly, slapped his hands on his thighs and looked at her with sudden seriousness. 'I haven't come bearing gifts for no apparent reason,' he said gravely.

'I had no idea that the doughnuts were meant to be a gift,' Jess replied politely. 'My birthday isn't for another three months, as it happens, but I appreciate the thought.'

'It's not so much a gift as more of a…how shall I put it…?'

'Please don't be coy, Curtis. That's not like you.'

He grinned and stood up and strolled over to her fridge, which he opened so that he could peer inside. 'Would you like to make me some breakfast?' he asked. 'Somehow doughnuts don't quite do the trick. Or I could make you something. What have you got?' He pulled out a yoghurt pot and inspected the lid. 'Aside from some Greek yoghurt three days past its sell-by date?'

This, Jess thought helplessly, was where being *good friends* got a girl. A guy who felt comfortable rooting through your fridge in search of food as opposed to the guy who showed up with red roses and tickets to the opera.

'Sit down. I guess I could do some eggs.'

'Or, better still, I could take you out for breakfast...'

'I can't,' she said hurriedly. 'I have a busy day ahead.'

'So you've said, even though you're not working this week. Busy doing what?'

'Meeting some of the staff,' she said vaguely, 'to discuss what else we can do to raise money for the school. There's a real risk it might be merged with the really huge secondary five miles away, which would be a disaster.'

'You need a generous donor,' Curtis murmured thoughtfully, but she was already turning away, fetching eggs and bread and concocting a breakfast she hadn't banked on making.

'So...' she said a few moments later as she plated up for both of them—scrambled eggs and toast. 'What do you have to ask me, Curtis?'

There was a reason he was sitting at her table, sprawled in the chair, watching her with those amazing cut glass green eyes. He wanted something and the very fact that he was beating about the bush was not a good sign.

'I need something of a…ah…a favour…'

'What?' She looked at him briefly, then back at her egg as a shiver of awareness threatened to bring way too much tell-tale colour to her cheeks. She'd always been aware of him but never so much as now. The fine balance between friendship and illicit, forbidden attraction had tipped far and fast into the illicit, forbidden attraction side, and the friendship element was struggling to keep pace.

'I'm best man at a wedding in two weeks' time. John Jones, a youthful Lord, as it happens. Have you heard of him?'

'Are you going to get to the point?'

'What would I do without you?' He grinned and reached forward and absently stroked her wrist with his finger.

An unthinking gesture and yet it fired up a response in her that was terrifyingly dramatic. She felt dampness pool between her legs and her breasts were suddenly heavy, her nipples stiff with a tingling sensation. Had he touched her before? Of course he had. A hug on her birthday, a peck on the cheek at Christmas. Once, and she burned when she remembered this, a kiss on the lips when they had been caught out under the mistletoe. She had been nineteen, he twenty-two. Afterwards he had pulled back and laughed and everyone around them had clapped but that kiss had burned for weeks afterwards.

If she'd wised up a little earlier to just how deep she had dived when it came to Curtis Hamilton she might have got her act together a little sooner instead of something like an engagement having to force her to confront her issues.

She subtly removed her hand and knew that he actually hadn't noticed that evasive withdrawal.

'So?' she asked politely, but her heart was still thumping and her skin was still tingling because her body had, just for a minute, gone AWOL.

'The point is that I want you to come with me.'

'You want me to come with you? I'm not following.'

'The invite includes a plus one,' Curtis explained, 'and I want you to be my plus one.' He looked away briefly before returning the full glare of his undivided attention to her.

'Why?'

'I think it would be nice for you,' he replied smoothly, his slow smile so coaxing, so seductive, so...*tempting* that Jess had to count to ten to clear her head.

'Nice for me...' she parroted, for want of anything better to say.

'As you've told me several times in the space of...' he made a show of consulting his luxury watch '...a little over an hour, you've been run ragged, barely able to function.'

'I don't think I actually used those words,' Jess pointed out, a little dazed.

'It's easy to become disillusioned with one's profession when you find yourself in a position of having no leisure time to yourself. There's a thin line between positivity at all hands to the tiller in a moment of crisis to negativity at the suspicion that you're being taken advantage of. And yes, I know you're going to tell me that you've been out and about on dates...' he paused, left a door ajar through which he invited her to step; Jess ignored him and he continued with a concerned sigh '...but you've barely stopped recently. I know that because

William mentioned you haven't been coming as often to help out with the memoirs...'

'Yes, I admit I've been busy but...'

'But nothing, Jess. You need a break and I'm here to provide just such a break for you. One weekend and it'll be somewhere you'll love...'

'Curtis, I can't just...'

'Courchevel.' He produced that with a flourish, like a magician producing a rabbit from a hat. 'A much-deserved weekend away at a lavish, all-expenses-paid five-star hotel doing the one thing in the world you love doing most. Skiing. Additionally, you'd be doing me a huge favour, Jess. You know my thoughts on weddings...'

'Yes,' Jess retorted with sarcasm, 'you think you're going to be a number one target for women with dreams of happy-ever-afters brought on by wedding contagion.'

'Exactly. I need you there to make the whole damn experience more bearable. A couple of hours I can deal with, but four days might become a little challenging.'

'You want a chaperone, in other words.'

A chaperone he knew wouldn't be foolish enough to get any wild ideas in her head—a chaperone who was a good pal and therefore immune to all thoughts of happy-ever-afters with a guy like him.

'And, tempting though you make it sound, Curtis Hamilton, the answer is an emphatic *no!*'

CHAPTER TWO

'WHY NOT?'

He looked genuinely startled and Jess could understand why. In his well-organised world, she had her place. She was his friend, probably the only woman on the planet he could count on as being his *friend*, with no annoying, unwelcome agenda. Why on earth, he was probably wondering, would she flatly reject his offer of an all-expenses-paid holiday which would give her a real battery-recharge after months of hard work trying to raise funds for the school?

She hadn't even bothered to offer any kind of explanation! She had rejected his offer out of hand.

He would be even more bewildered at the fact that she had turned down the chance *to ski*. She adored skiing and was so good that she could instruct.

While she struggled to come up with a

plausible explanation, his face cleared and he looked at her knowingly.

'I get it,' he murmured.

'You do?' Jess queried, alarmed.

'I do. We've known each other a long time, Jess. I can read you like a book.'

Alarm blossomed into panic. He was shrewd when it came to reading undercurrents. Show him a signal barely visible to the naked eye, and he could ferret out what it meant in a matter of seconds. Had all her dodging and evasion pointed him in the very direction she had been so desperate to conceal? Had he gleaned, somehow, that she was *attracted* to him? That their so-called platonic friendship, which he treasured, was something she longed to take several steps further.

Had he guessed how she truly felt about him?

She blanched. Honestly, she could think of nothing worse. It wasn't just the mortification, it wasn't just the thought of him laughing his head off at the thought of her actually imagining that she might be competition for the glamorous blondes he was fond of dating... *No*, it would be the loss of friendship that went with that because he would run a mile in the opposite direction.

'You can?' she asked weakly and he nodded.

'You've hit the dating scene big time,' he expanded. 'The fact that you're so secretive about it, secretive about your hot date last night, is telling me something.'

'What is it telling you?'

'It's serious.'

He waited. She failed to embellish so he continued, a little jerkily. 'Frankly, I'm a little hurt that you don't feel you can confide in me.' Surprisingly, he *did* feel hurt and...what else? A feeling of edginess that nestled on the periphery of what seemed acceptable to him. He dismissed the uneasy feeling quickly.

'Why should I confide in you about my private life?' Jess asked, sounding genuinely puzzled.

'You know all about mine!'

'Curtis, so does half the country.' She burst out laughing, expecting him to follow suit, but he stared at her with such a disgruntled expression that she carried on laughing, couldn't help herself. 'You're in the tabloids more often than the daily weather reports,' she said wryly. 'You don't actually need to tell me who you're seeing because all I have to do is grab a newspaper from the corner shop.'

Her stomach tightened but she kept smiling. Yes, she saw all those cute, tiny blondes he went out with. None seemed to last longer than ten minutes.

He said that he was an open book. Was he though? When she thought about it, there were huge gaps in her knowledge about him. He'd never spoken about his childhood, aside from to tell her in passing that he could not have hoped for a better father figure than William. He was adept at deflecting questions he didn't want to answer and questions that were too probing were adroitly side-stepped.

He was approaching thirty and, yes, young enough to be wary of being tied down, but when he talked about women and relationships there had always been an edge of cynicism in his voice, a flat determination that marriage was an institution he had no time for.

And yet he had been engaged. He hadn't been the one to break it off. Had a broken heart accounted for his aversion to commitment? Jess could swear that he had never wanted to be tied down, that he had always been wary of commitment…or was that just her imagination playing tricks on her?

'You never really told me what happened between you and Caitlin,' Jess said, treading on ground previously untrodden. She'd tentatively asked at the time but hadn't pursued the matter when he'd failed to explain. Yet weren't they supposed to be great *friends*?

Well, this friendship wasn't exactly on a par when he felt hurt because she had chosen not to blurt out everything about her private life but *she* was handed precious little real information about *his*.

Suddenly, she felt the stirrings of an anger she had never felt towards him before. Her anger ratcheted up a notch or two when he stilled because clearly he wanted that untrodden ground to remain untrodden.

'That business with Caitlin is ancient history,' he dismissed in a guarded tone.

The question had come at him from left field and Curtis shifted uncomfortably. For a few seconds he seemed to look down into deep, dark water that swirled lazily beneath him, so full of things unspoken and buried sadness.

'I must say, Curtis,' Jess mused sweetly, 'that it's a bit rich for you to feel hurt because I happen to want to keep my private life to myself, when you have no qualms about keeping *your* private life to yourself. The whole world knows what women you date because you don't mind them knowing, but you're very good at keeping yourself to yourself when it comes to making sure no one oversteps the mark...'

'Okay. Spit it out. What's going on, Jess?'

'Nothing. I'm just pointing out the obvious.'

'So you don't want to tell me who you're seeing?' He shrugged with exaggerated indifference. 'So be it. It's not the end of the world.'

That stung. She hated the feeling. It had been bearable keeping her distance, thinking about him but building up her immunity, but now that he was sitting across from her she *missed* their easy familiarity.

His suddenly unreadable green eyes were locked speculatively on her face and she felt her heart speed up. She wanted to cry, which was ridiculous because it was perfectly healthy for her to keep her distance. In time, they would resume their friendship but when that happened she would no longer be in thrall to him.

'I'm assuming,' he drawled, 'that that's your reason for turning down my generous offer...'

What to say? How to respond? She thought about her 'hot date'. Poor Mike...so nice, so pleasant-looking—so many boxes ticked—and yet not enough.

That was information she didn't want to impart so she shrugged but, instead of backing away from the topic, he shamelessly prodded, 'Well? Am I on the right track here?'

'How is it,' she said, frustrated, 'that I never realised how much like a dog with a bone you are when it comes to getting what you want?'

He visibly relaxed and she was cravenly grateful that the status quo was back.

'I have no idea. You should have. Are you concerned that the new guy in your life might not like the fact that we're spending a long weekend together?'

Jess marvelled that he could make a statement of fact sound so disconcertingly intimate without even realising it.

'I would never let anyone dictate how I spend my time,' she retorted and blushed when he grinned with smug approval.

'Thought not, but if that *had* been the case then you could truthfully have told him that we would be in separate rooms and, quite honestly, you would be free to more or less do your own thing for most of the weekend. Yes, we would be together for the ceremony, but that's about it. You could ski to your heart's content the rest of the time...' He leant towards her and murmured softly, 'Don't tell me that you're not tempted...'

Jess blinked.

Temptation was a finger's touch away if he but knew it and when it came to temptation the prospect of skiing paled in comparison.

'But,' he continued briskly, 'just in case you need further persuasion, I would very much like to dangle a carrot in front of you...'

'What carrot?'

'A very healthy donation to your school.' He

smiled. 'I know that if it's not because of a guy, then it must be because you don't think you'll be able to spare the time because you're all engaged on a fundraising drive to get new desks for your school...'

'Computer equipment.'

'I already contribute generously to many charities via my various business holdings, but I would like to personally donate towards whatever equipment you need.'

He named a sum that took her breath away because not only would it cover all the equipment the school needed, but also repair work to two of the buildings caused by water damage the previous winter.

'It's *that* important for you to have a chaperone to a wedding, Curtis?'

'You should have come to me if you needed financial assistance for your school.'

'Of course I'm not going to do that!'

'Why not?'

'Because I... I just *wouldn't*.'

'You're one of a kind, Jess,' he said softly. 'You have no idea how many people would think nothing of coming to me with a begging bowl to support whatever cause they needed money for. You're one of the least opportunistic women I've ever known.'

Pleasure bloomed inside her and she pinkened.

'We go back a long way,' she admitted. 'I knew you before you made it big.'

'So will you come with me, Jess? You really would be doing me a huge favour...'

There were no other reasons she could possibly give for rejecting his offer. They weren't on the same page emotionally, but how was he to know that?

And if she kept avoiding him, surely he would begin to smell a rat? She valued his friendship. She would hate to lose it and she knew that in due course, once she'd broken free of whatever spell he had cast over her down the years, they would once again be pals, but this time on an equal footing.

Would she now want to jeopardise that? Mike the teacher might not have been the one for her, but there *was* someone out there for her and when that someone came into her life all the foolish feelings she had towards Curtis would disappear like dew in the summer sun.

That was the way life worked.

And, additionally, it now struck her, maybe it *would* be a good idea to go on that skiing weekend. Maybe a burst of Curtis would get him out of her system once and for all. Maybe seeing him in fits and starts over the years had fed her infatuation. Maybe a weekend in his company would do the trick when it came to stifling all the inappropriate feelings she still seemed to harbour towards him. She would see firsthand, in the presence of all the beautiful, eligible women who would be there, just how out of reach he was for someone like her. She would be firmly reminded of her status as *friend.*

It was exhausting thinking about all the permutations of the situation. A simple invitation and she'd been thrown into a tailspin that was giving her a headache.

'The school *would* benefit from your kind generosity,' she agreed. 'I'll come but please don't think that you have to stick to your promise about the money. You're right. It would be nice to relax and to ski.'

Curtis smiled, satisfied. 'I'm a man of my word,' he told her. 'By tomorrow evening your school's bank account will be considerably healthier...'

* * *

Jess managed to keep her head firmly down over the next week and a half. The money which he had donated to the school was so greatly appreciated that she thought the governors might actually declare a day's holiday in celebration.

When she knew that he had returned to London, three days after having arrived to see his godfather, she cycled over to William, where news of her weekend's escapade had reached his ears.

'I'm thrilled for you,' he confided as they sat at his kitchen table with a plate of homemade scones between them and Earl Grey in cups. 'You're just like Curtis. You work too hard, my dear.' He looked at her shrewdly and then asked whether whatever chap she might be going out with wouldn't object to her accompanying a man for a weekend away.

'So far—' she laughed '—I've been on three dates with three guys and, as the song goes, William, I'm still looking...'

'There's always my godson,' William returned with a sly twinkle in his eye and she coloured like a beetroot.

'Don't be ridiculous,' she huffed in an un-naturally high voice. 'Curtis is my friend and *that's all.*' She cleared her throat, looked at her phone for the time and shifted her eyes away from his piercing blue ones. 'We might be going to this wedding together, but it's only because he's scared that some scheming cute blonde with wedding rings in her sight might make a beeline for him…'

'He does enjoy his cute blondes, not that any of them ever seem to work out…'

'He's a commitment-phobe, William.'

'You think so, my dear? I would say he wants commitment more than he thinks. He's just in the process of making his way to the right recipient.'

'I should get going.' She stood up, began putting on her thick padded coat. She didn't dare glance in William's direction. Had boredom got the better of him? Made his imagination a little too overactive for his own good?

She would put him in touch with a few clubs as soon as she got back to Ely. She knew a lot of people and she could think of some very nice organisations that would welcome a clever retired lecturer who was also a fantastic cook.

Was he too confirmed a bachelor to think about letting a suitable lady into his life? It would certainly distract him from a life without the routine of his university lecturing job.

Left to his own devices, the last thing she needed was for him to start second-guessing how she felt about Curtis.

'There's a lot more to my godson than meets the eye.' He patted her arm fondly as he walked her to the door. 'There are a lot of hidden depths there, my dear.'

'I'll bear that in mind,' Jess replied, laughing, 'when I see him forcing himself not to flirt with all the women who will be flinging themselves at him at the wedding.'

Hidden depths? Sure, many times she had wondered at what stirred under the surface of his easy charm. She knew nothing about him prior to when he had joined her school, and now William's murmured words had unleashed questions in her head she knew had always been there...

The last thing she needed at this juncture was curiosity, which was on an equal level with nervousness when it came to something else she didn't need, but she was still as nervous as a kitten when, bags packed and long weekend in sight, she pushed her way through the crowds at Heathrow to spy him lounging by the First-class check-in, looking at something on his phone.

Every single time Jess saw him, it was as though she were seeing him for the very first time. He was always just so much more dramatic than she remembered.

He looked effortlessly cool in a beaten leather motorbike jacket, faded jeans, black sweater and sturdy tan loafers. On the ground was a luxury case. He looked up at her approach and straightened.

'Thank you for the driver, Curtis.' She launched into speech to still the butterflies in her tummy. In her layers of bulky clothing she felt frumpy and unexciting.

'I wouldn't dream of putting you through the hassle of getting on public transport. You should get yourself a car, Jess.'

'I already have a car.'

He wasn't looking at her. He had relieved her of her passport and had flipped it open to inspect her picture, while she tried not to cringe because it was a stunningly unflattering one taken when she still wore thick specs and was just a little too overweight to be called voluptuous.

'Mmm. I was talking about one that works when you want it to work instead of when it feels like it.' He checked his watch. 'Not much time to kick around here. It's going to be a long trip. No idea why I didn't take the jet.' He eyed her. 'Very good idea that you chose to wear comfy clothes.'

'You should see the stuff I've packed,' Jess said, walking fast to keep pace even though she was only a few inches shorter than him.

'Including to wear to the wedding?'

'Yes, Curtis. Jogging bottoms and a sweat-shirt. Is there a problem with that?'

This was the banter she was accustomed to, light-hearted conversation between friends, but she could breathe him in as he walked alongside her and when she glanced across she was achingly aware of the leather jacket, the tight jeans encasing his muscular legs, the stubble on his chin, the thickness of his slightly too long hair.

'You'll have to excuse my lack of chit-chat, Jess. I have a hell of a lot of work to do on the plane. My routine was thrown out because I hung around for a bit longer than I'd planned with William. Kept an eye on him, by the way. He seems in good humour and…' he slanted his green eyes across to her; there was an amused half smile tugging his mouth and Jess felt her breath hitch in her throat because he was just so damned *sexy* '…he seems curiously excited at the prospect of us spending a long weekend together.'

Jess didn't know what to say to that, but she was spared having to make any response because he was obviously in a hurry to get down to work.

He cut a swathe through the crowds, oblivious to the heads swinging in their direction. He oozed sex appeal. Tall, commanding, movie star looks with an apparent lack of vanity that his whole urgent body language implied without him having to work at it.

No wonder he had women flocking to him in droves.

She still didn't know exactly what had happened between him and Caitlin, but if he'd had his heart broken it was no wonder he wanted to deflect any unwanted hopefuls who might want to target him at the wedding. Once bitten would definitely be twice shy.

They hit the First-class lounge at a brisk pace.

'Coffee...tea...food...pastries... Take your pick, Jess.' He wasn't looking at her as he said this. He was making a beeline towards a nest of deep chairs surrounding a low table, already pulling out his laptop, so at ease in her company that there was no attempt to disguise the fact that he intended to spend the time working until their flight was called. She would have to do her own thing and that suited her just fine.

'Want anything?' She dumped her bag on the table and remained standing as he sat down, briefly looking up at her.

'Nothing. I'll be a little less antisocial just as soon as I've answered this string of emails.'

'I don't expect you to socialise with me, Curtis.' She began unzipping the puffer jacket. Thoughts crowded into her head and she fought against them—thoughts she'd never seemed to have had before, or at least acknowledged. Mean, spiky thoughts that he would be making a mammoth effort to socialise with her if she'd been one of his dainty blondes. He didn't see the need to put himself out when it came to her because there was just too much familiarity between them.

'What do you mean?' For the first time since she'd arrived he actually focused on her, his sea-green eyes riveted to her face.

'I mean—' Jess cleared her throat '—I know why I'm here.' She hoped she sounded airy and wryly amused. She feared she might just sound defensive and a little hurt. 'I'm here to protect you from the fan club waiting to get their claws into you.'

'Bit of an exaggeration.' But he grinned, eyebrows shooting up as he relaxed back to focus fully on her with lazy, lingering amusement.

A prickle of heat coursed through her and she abruptly turned away with a shrug. 'I've brought my laptop and some schoolwork I'll have to get through because I'm taking a couple of days off. I have more than enough to occupy myself while you work.'

He looked at her. What was he missing here?

He hadn't seen her in a while, but it wasn't the first time that weeks had elapsed without contact. Wasn't that the nature of good friendships? Time could pass but catching up was always seamless.

Except this time…

This time something was a little off-kilter, although for the life of him he couldn't work out what it was.

Surely she wasn't offended because he'd offered her an all-expenses-paid free trip to Courchevel where, aside from a few hours in a frock drinking champagne and chit-chatting with a few people, she would endure nothing more gruelling than eating great food, drinking fine wine and skiing down some of the most invigorating slopes in the world?

What was there not to like in that scenario?

He uneasily wondered whether she was miffed because there was a limit to how far he would go when it came to confiding.

When he thought about it, she'd been a bit odd ever since the Caitlin fiasco. He absently watched her. She was taller than most of the women in the vicinity, her body concealed underneath a navy-blue jumper that reached to mid-thigh, where it merged into the navy-blue jeans and navy-blue trainers.

It was a revelation actually seeing her eyes,

though. Deep, deep blue. He'd never noticed how unusual they were behind those thick spectacles she used to wear.

In front of him his laptop blinked, demanding his attention, but his mind was stubbornly drifting as he tried to get a grip on what it was that jarred.

No one knew the full story about the disaster he had narrowly avoided. Despite his openness when it came to the women he dated, despite his willingness to allow the paparazzi to peer into his life, he knew that he rigorously controlled what the public knew about him and the truth was that, despite the parade of women and his willingness to be photographed with them, he was intensely private.

He frowned. The past was a place he never visited. It was too dark and there was no point. Information about him was scant on the Internet. It worked being open to all intents and purposes because it meant that no one really had any interest in delving beyond what was on the table and he liked it that way.

It had not occurred to him that he could or should explain the situation with his ex to anyone. Even William knew precious little. The

story was that he'd been dumped by a beautiful woman who'd become bored with him. He
was very happy to leave it there.

He shifted. He was uncomfortable with this
bout of introspection and bemused that the
woman now helping herself to coffee had managed to bring it on.

Still brooding over an atmosphere he couldn't
quite put his finger on, he watched as she spun
round and began walking carefully towards
him, coffee in one hand and a bottle of water
in the other. She should have just got waiter
service but that wouldn't have occurred to her,
which made him smile.

Just like that, she looked across to him and
their eyes met and tangled and for a few seconds his breath caught sharply in his throat.
But then he smiled more broadly as she neared,
easing back into the low chair, ready to tease
her about helping herself to coffee when there
were eager attendants waiting to do it for their
privileged customers, ready to share a wry
joke about the quality of the delicacies on offer
being as good as in any restaurant, ready to
ask her why she hadn't helped herself to any
of the sweet morsels. He knew from old that

she loved nothing more than a slice of cake or a chocolate bar.

But then she leant forward to deposit the water and the coffee on the table and in one smooth movement, straightened to remove the bulky sweater.

And he stared.

It was rare for him to be disconcerted to the extent that he was rendered speechless, but in this instance he was because the figure on display underneath that shapeless blue sweater was…definitely not what he'd expected.

He had a moment of pure confusion at the dichotomy between the reality of what he was seeing and his memory of her hiding behind her thick specs and untidy hair and shapeless garments. Wasn't she just the tiniest bit over-weight? She had been…hadn't she?

The specs had gone and the hair was gloriously shiny, falling in dark waves to her shoulders, and her body…

He was shocked by the dramatic response of his body. Since when was he in the habit of losing control? He made a futile attempt to drag his eyes away but for a few seconds all he could take in, as she leant to shove the jumper into the holdall, was the sway of her full breasts, the rounded curve of her hips and legs that were incredibly long and surprisingly slender. She brushed her hair away from her face, tucking it behind her ear. She wasn't looking at him and he concluded that that was a relief because she would have been startled to see how compulsively he was staring, but he just couldn't seem to help himself.

When had *that* happened? When had she turned into a sex siren? Why hadn't she given him any prior warning as to what to expect? He really hadn't seen much of her at all over the past few months and it dawned on him that this body transformation was in line with her sudden exploration of the dating scene. It was a sobering thought. She wasn't one of these hard-edged women who knew how the world turned when it came to guys! She was...well, she was *Jess*! Sweetly innocent and endearingly straightforward.

He thought about her with some sex-crazed guy on the lookout for a one-night stand and congratulated himself on the surge of protectiveness that smothered him just for a few destabilising seconds.

'Is there something on my face?'

'Come again?'

'You're staring.'

He flushed darkly, shifted, scowled.

'Mind was a million miles away.' His voice was more abrupt than he'd intended and he saw her face tighten with hurt but, caught out as he had been, the last thing on his mind was an apology. 'Work,' he offered, staring at his laptop while his mind tried to compute a shift inside himself that he didn't care for.

'Okay.'

He heard her laugh and was aware of her sitting down again and reaching for the coffee. All he could see in his mind was the abundance of luscious breasts straining against the stretchy black fabric of her skin-tight T-shirt.

It could not have been a more modest garment, with a high, round neck and long enough to ensure not even a sliver of stomach was revealed, however much she twisted, turned and stretched. And the jeans encasing those long, long legs? Blue denim without a designer label in sight, and high-waisted enough to pretty much classify as unfashionable in most of the circles he mixed in, and yet she could not have looked sexier.

'I should go sit at one of those desks.' He nodded to the bank of desks by the wall, with all the accoutrements for hooking up to the Internet. He tried to kill the uncomfortable flush of discomfort and the zinging awareness of her looking at him with those surprisingly beautiful almond-shaped navy eyes. 'Charging banks,' he muttered. 'Useful.'

'Sure.'

The smile was frozen on her face as he stalked off without a backward glance.

Could he have made it any clearer that he couldn't be bothered with her company?

Was this a terrible mistake? Was their friendship only workable when they met in passing? They weren't kids any more, sitting on the sofa and watching movies with a bag of popcorn between them. Life had separated them. Life and experiences. Was she jeopardising what they had by being here? Some things that thrived in a certain environment wilted and died in another.

They were so close, she mused, pointedly

not looking in his direction but fishing into her bag for her laptop, and yet there was a gulf between them that had become glaringly apparent in the wake of his relationship and engagement to Caitlin.

First-hand, she had seen how the important stuff had never been shared. She knew precious little about his past and nothing at all about how he really felt about…love and marriage and parenthood or anything else that really mattered.

He was the least likely guy she should ever have had a crush on, never mind nurturing deeper feelings that would never be returned.

Maybe he was regretting inviting her along for four days of together time.

Maybe she should tell him that he should feel free to ditch her if he wanted. It wasn't as though she would lose sleep if she missed a wedding where she knew no one!

She would wait and see how things played out but already she longed for the safety of her little terraced house and the peace of not having her feelings challenged.

CHAPTER THREE

THE HOTEL—WHICH, Curtis had told her en route, had been hand-picked by his PA—was one of those dreamy locations only within reach of someone with extremely deep pockets.

Unlike most of the hotels, this one was more like someone's private country house. Neither of them had brought skis, in her case because she didn't actually own any, but she had given her shoe size a couple of days ago to his secretary and not only were skis waiting for her but also boots in exactly the right size.

They were ushered into a foyer warm with subdued earth-toned colours. An expanse of cream and caramel marble led to a desk behind which two smiling women, who would not have been out of place on the cover of a fashion magazine, were waiting to check them in.

Despite the fact that it wasn't an adults-only

hotel, there was a marked absence of any families. Jess was so accustomed to sharing her space with kids of all ages and sizes that she found herself whispering, the way she would in a library.

'Lovely.' This to Curtis as they stood in front of the blonde magazine cover receptionist who was busily trying not to pay the slightest bit of attention to the hunk standing in front of her.

'You're whispering,' he whispered with a grin. 'You approve then…?'

Checked in, he took the credit-card-style keys handed to him without glancing in the direction of the receptionist, instead gazing at Jess, eyes still amused.

'It's certainly a step up from the last place I went to with the school kids,' she said crisply. Those green eyes on her did crazy things to her breathing and she broke eye contact to look around. It was awe-inspiring. Where he had grown up, if not in the lap of luxury then in the lap of well-to-do comfort, *she* had been brought up with the motto that *Every penny counts*. Her contact with any kind of luxury had been all those many times she had hung out at his godfather's place while her mother had cleaned, bringing in some pin money to bolster the salary her dad got from the glass factory where he worked as a foreman.

She'd never in her entire life ever imagined that somewhere as perfect as this could possibly exist. It was a prime example of what happened when a top interior designer shook hands with limitless budget.

'Have you been here before?'

'Every year,' Curtis said wryly. 'I like the fact that it's small and it's private. One of the advantages to having money. It buys you peace, if that's what you're after.'

'Is that why we're here?' she asked shrewdly.

She dragged her eyes away from the breathtaking surroundings, reminding herself that there would be ample time for her to explore on her own at some point, and looked at him as the concealed lift pinged shut behind them with the hush of bank vault doors softly sealing closed.

Suddenly the space felt suffocatingly intimate and her skin heated up as he continued to look at her.

'We're in separate rooms,' he said. 'Adjoining thanks to a connecting door, but separate.

Bearing in mind you're supposed to be my plus one, it made sense not to advertise the fact that we're not sleeping together. My plus ones would usually share my bed.'

Jess could feel her skin begin to burn and her breathing became jerky and shallow because, just like that, her head was cluttered with images of him in bed, naked...

She gulped and her eyes glazed over and thankfully she was spared a response because the lift doors slid open, disgorging them into a plush hall off which their rooms were located.

'Your key.'

Jess took the card and stared at it for a few seconds while her batteries tried to recharge.

'Good idea,' she muttered, turning away and blindly tapping the door with the card to push it open, at which point she turned to him, finally braving his eyes, with the safety of her bedroom behind her. 'No point...you know... wagging tongues and the like...'

'My thoughts exactly.'

Jess wondered whether it was her imagination or did those veiled eyes remain on her for just a tiny bit longer than necessary? At any rate, there was a furnace raging inside her and she couldn't wait to douse it under a tepid shower.

'So...' It wasn't yet six in the evening.

'So?' He'd been lounging against the door-frame, having edged her back without her even noticing, but now he straightened, one hundred per cent business. 'Tonight I'm meeting John and a handful of the guys for a night of fun and too much alcohol, I imagine. You're free to do your own thing. Order whatever you want, explore the place to your heart's content. Everything is on me, Jess. You can buy the entire boutique downstairs if you want to. Alternatively, you can come with me and hang with the bride-to-be and her bridesmaids, who will be doing their own thing, probably with considerably more restraint. I'm sure Philippa wouldn't object...'

'I'll skip that option,' Jess said hurriedly.

'Thought you might. Right. And tomorrow... what say we take to the slopes? Before the rest of the world has time to wake up?'

'Isn't that going to be difficult if you're nursing a hangover?' But that sounded just about right to her. She knew that he was a good skier. There would be no awkward conversations on the slopes and the truth was that she was dying to get her skis on and get out there. She'd gazed at the conditions from the back seat of the limo that had ferried them to their hotel and the snow was perfect. Mouth-wateringly perfect.

'I have way too much self-control to over-indulge in alcohol,' he informed her. And it was true. He'd spent too many years knowing what it felt like to have no control over any single part of his life, however minuscule. It was thus the one thing he valued now. 'I've never been drunk in my life before and it's not a habit I have any intention of picking up any time soon. So are you okay to fend for yourself this evening?'

'You're a saint, Curtis,' she teased, relaxed at the thought of an evening to herself and normality being resumed in the morning on the slopes. 'And yes, I think I can manage. I've been doing it for the past twenty-six years after all.'

She thought that she might have spent the evening with her thoughts on him, brooding on whatever the next couple of days held in store and analysing to the point of a migraine whether she regretted her decision to come or not, but in fact she had never felt so relaxed as she unwound over the next few hours.

How long must it have been since she'd had time off? Ages. When her dad had died quite suddenly, her mother had been plunged into the sort of pervasive depression that had cast a cloud over every aspect of Jess's life. Her social life had been put on hold because making sure her mother was okay had demanded most of her spare time. Holidays of any sort had not just been put on hold—they'd been relegated to the deep freezer, from which they hadn't emerged to see the light of day.

Now, she felt like a kid in a sweet shop. She explored the hotel from top to bottom, marvelling at the subterranean labyrinth of steam grottos and saunas, practically enough for each guest to have his or her own. Then there was the indoor pool, carved out to mimic an underground lagoon, complete with a wall of cascading water and a jacuzzi.

There was a comprehensive gym and a Michelin starred restaurant, as well as two further casual dining areas, two bars and a spa, which she peeked into. It smelled of sandal-wood and eucalyptus.

By the time she'd ordered room service, she'd forgotten all about the stresses that had been plaguing her over the past few weeks and months.

Her bedroom suite was the last word in lux-ury, with a sitting room that managed to be comfortable yet scarily perfect and an en suite bathroom with a bath the size of an Olympic swimming pool, in which she luxuriated for a ridiculous length of time.

There were floor-to-ceiling windows every-where, a clever bit of design that allowed you to look out at the snowy wonderland, an un-impeded vista of white.

The following morning her phone pinged, and she smiled when she read Curtis's text saying that he would be waiting for her in Reception.

Breakfast in bed and then a day on the slopes before the ceremony the following day at the groom's parents' ski lodge, which was appar-ently more than big enough for the party of nearly a hundred people, a string quartet, a sprawling buffet and all the other stuff that was part and parcel of an aristocratic wedding.

Since she had only ever attended three weddings—none of which were fancier than the local church and, in one case, a marquee on the village green, which had been brilliant—Jess couldn't wait to see how the other half celebrated.

But for now…

She felt an illicit thrill at the thought of seeing Curtis. Forgotten were the edge-of-seat nerves and the back and forth wondering what she was doing.

She'd only bought one new thing for the trip and that was her ski outfit—a reckless splurge but when next would she be in a position like this?

At a little after nine she headed down to Reception, having fully togged up for the day ahead.

Outside the snow was freshly fallen so she was looking forward to some grippy turns and a smooth ride down the excellent pistes. She knew that sometimes the cushion of snow could be powdery enough to make her feel as though she was floating and nothing was more magical.

He was there.

They matched. All black. Her heart thumped as she strolled towards him.

She felt exposed in the ski outfit, which clung to her like a second skin. Had he seen her in anything that hadn't been baggy? Yes, surely so, but in the past few months she'd slimmed considerably and never had she been more conscious of her figure.

Looking up from his phone, Curtis inhaled sharply, eyes narrowing on her as she sashayed towards him.

Because no other word could describe the sexy motion of her hips. Her legs went on and on *and on* and where the heck had she got that outfit? It contoured a body that men's dreams were made of and his legendary fondness for petite blondes disappeared under a haze of lust that leapt out at him and sent a charge of high voltage electricity racing through his body with mercurial ferocity.

He hardened, his body's immediate response, yet one that he could not remember having ever experienced in his life before with such urgency. When it came to the game of seduction he was *always* the one in charge. This time, however, his body was calling the shots and it was infuriating.

What the hell was going on? This woman was his closest female friend—his *only* female friend! He'd never subscribed to the homily that a man couldn't be friends with a woman without sex rearing its ugly head. He'd always known that he had far too much self-control for that sort of indiscriminate response to ever hold sway.

He knew he was staring but he couldn't seem to help himself and his mouth was dry.

And the rest of his body was making him wonder whether he'd ever had an attack of plain old-fashioned lust.

Black outfit, zip running from waist to neck, outlining the most perfect breasts he'd ever seen. Breasts that were much more than a handful and those shapely legs encased in tight black and tucked into white boots.

Her sunglasses were propped on her forehead, as his were.

'Ready?' he half croaked, spinning round

on his heel because, despite the two sets of thermals and the trousers, he was very much afraid that she might catch sight of his rampant erection.

'Can't wait,' Jess carolled. She looped her arm through his. 'Tell me how your evening went,' she encouraged when he failed to say anything further. 'I did wonder whether I should text you to find out whether you were in one piece…'

'As you can see—' he couldn't look at her, couldn't risk prolonging his rampant response '—I don't do overindulgence when it comes to alcohol. The plan today—' he could hardly detach his arm but the weight of hers wound through his was just adding to his mental disarray, so focusing on a businesslike discussion of the day ahead seemed a good idea '—is some skiing and then a quick lunch. I have work to do after lunch, so you are free to do your own thing. At six, we're going to John's chalet for a pre-wedding dinner. It'll be informal. No need to dress up.' He had a pang of nostalgia for her uniform of baggy clothes, which had always been so good at concealing her figure. 'You've lost weight.' He deviated sharply from the conversation he had had in mind, and cast a quick glance across at her.

'A bit.'

'Hope you haven't joined those women who think that eating anything that isn't raw or can't be grown in a vegetable patch is a crime...'

'Far from it,' Jess countered politely, removing her arm and focusing on the business of the skiing ahead, because something in his voice was edgy and just a little bit...offensive. Although she couldn't quite put her finger on it because it was the usual sort of teasing remark she would have expected from him.

Did he think that she should somehow have been happy to remain as the five ten, over-weight girl next door hiding behind her spectacles and her untamed hair?

She banked down a sudden attack of self-consciousness because she knew she looked just fine. The outfit suited her and if he didn't like it, which was the implication in his voice, then too bad.

The slopes were already busy, but this part of the world was classy when it came to skiing. There were so many ski lifts that no one ever had to wait, and the ski instructors were sometimes ex-world champions.

She was in her element here. There were no kids around to channel and supervise and cajole and tell off for horsing around. An opportunity like this would never come her way again and she was *not* going to let Curtis Hamilton spoil it because he seemed to think that she had no right to try and change.

There was only one way to deal with that, she decided, and that was to pretend that he just wasn't there at all, and for the next three hours that was exactly what she did.

She let the white, snowy slopes cool her mind and she lost herself in the thrill of feeling cold air rushing against her face and the freedom that came with speed. He tried to outpace her but she kept up, enjoying the challenge, equal against equal, both savouring the same thrill that was blessed respite from the tangle of emotions that had been plaguing her for longer than she cared to think.

Buoyed, she declined to join him for lunch and instead told him that she would meet him in the foyer in time for the pre-wedding party.

'And yes,' she said, harking back to their pre-ski conversation, 'I know it's going to be an informal event this evening and I think I've brought just the right outfit to wear.' Which wasn't strictly true but there were shops out there and she was going to treat herself to something nice. So what if he preferred she stood still and never changed? She would make sure she chose something that would prove to him once and for all that she was no longer the girl next door, stuck in her predictable comfort zone.

'There's no need to go overboard.' He smiled a little stiffly. 'John's parents will be there and they couldn't be more old-fashioned.'

'What are you trying to say?'

'I'm not trying to say anything.' He raked his fingers through his hair and looked away. 'Right. If you're sure you won't join me for lunch, then I'll see you later. Six sharp. I have a driver to take us there and bring us back.'

An uncustomary sense of rebellion propelled Jess into boutiques she would never have dared venture into a handful of months before, when she was so self-conscious about her size that concealment had been the key factor when it came to choosing clothes.

She would never be able to compete with the tiny little Christmas tree baubles Curtis favoured but she was proud of her shape and wasn't going to hide it under layers of drab clothes. If Curtis had been implying that she should try and cover up because she wasn't skinny enough to wear tight clothes then he was in for a shock. She wondered whether seeing her in her skiing outfit had alarmed him and grinned when she thought about that.

What a prude underneath that charming libertine exterior! At least as far as *she* was concerned!

She reflected as she threw herself into an afternoon of shopping and to heck with counting her pennies, that we all ended up being stuck in categories and sometimes, when we wanted to get out, it was a whole lot more difficult than we expected.

She wondered where she would end up if she broke free of the category into which she had always been stuck as far as Curtis was concerned.

No longer the comfortable friend, but then what…?

Maybe still a friend but one who was allowed past all those No Trespass signs she realised he always had up, maybe a friend who could openly chat to him about her love life because she would have gone past her inconvenient infatuation to find herself a guy who really appreciated her. Maybe they would go on double dates together, although her imagination found it hard to stretch to that scenario.

At any rate, anything would be better than the limbo she felt she'd occupied for too long.

The only coat she had was a mid-thigh-length, very unbecoming but highly practical black down padded puffer, perfect for intensely wintry conditions. But she'd treated herself to a pair of low flat boots and a long-sleeved woollen dress in a flattering shade of deep blue, with its elegant cowl neck which managed to expose just the right amount of shoulder. It clung to her much like the ski outfit did but left a lot less to the imagination when it came to the length of her legs and the fullness of her breasts.

She was a big girl and she wasn't going to try and play it down.

She hugged herself as they stepped out to the waiting four-wheel drive limo. For a few seconds she breathed in the purity of the mountain air and enjoyed the tingling crispness of the dry cold on her cheeks.

'Beautiful, isn't it?' He paused alongside her, both staring out at the same stunning view of rolling peaks and valleys of purest white, even though it was dark. 'Glad you came?'

'It's been a lovely day skiing.' She moved away, letting herself into the back seat of the chauffeur-driven car and then shuffling along so that he could slide in next to her.

The stillness of everything outside, a stillness that only seemed to exist in the snow-capped silent mountains, seemed to trap them in an artificial intimacy and she hurried to break it by launching into frenetic small talk.

What was the lodge like where the ceremony was to be held? Had he been before? How many people would he know when they got there? Had he managed to get much work done? Had he spoken to his godfather? What a poppet William was...

She was hyper-aware of him next to her, within touching distance. His padded heavy-duty waterproof coat was as thick as hers but still she was acutely aware of his lean body underneath and as the car drew up to the lodge she breathed a sigh of relief. How much more inane chatting could she rustle up before he asked her whether she was feeling all right? If she veered any more wildly from making a point of showing him that everything was as normal as always between them to babbling nervously as if he'd suddenly turned into a stranger then he would definitely think she'd lost the plot.

The sight of the ski lodge, though, provided ample distraction. It was an immense pile, illuminated in a blaze of light and straddling the side of a snowy hill in various steps, with each layer fronted by an enormous wrap-around veranda. Five verandas. There were at least a dozen high-end cars parked in the courtyard, each of them snow-covered. To the side, away from the house and in the blackness, Curtis pointed out a helipad, which probably accounted for how many of the guests would arrive.

'I've always wondered how the other half live,' she murmured, sufficiently distracted not to notice the sexiness of his lazy smile in response or the flare of warmth in his eyes as he looked at her straining forward, mouth half open in awe. 'Now I know...'

'It pays its way,' he said wryly. 'It's impressive but it's rented out for most of the ski season and pretty much all of the summer, when it's really very beautiful here, even minus the snow...'

'I guess not many people can afford the upkeep of a place like this,' she sighed as the car purred to a stop.

'I can and I'm always very happy to acquaint you in other lessons about how the other half live,' he murmured, leaning towards her, his breath warm on her cheek, causing her to pull back in startled response.

Her eyes widened and for a second there were just the two of them in the back seat of the car and then she said urgently, to break the sudden electricity that seemed to have built up, 'I can't remember...we're not supposed to be an item, are we...?'

The driver had rushed out to open the passenger door for her, lest she do it herself, as she had earlier, and she stepped out and away from the radius of Curtis's overpowering personality.

'People will assume that we're going out.' He shrugged. 'I've told the guys that I'm here with a woman...so they've reached their own conclusions. People will see me with you and...'

'And all those pesky women will steer clear?'

'I don't need anyone imagining that I'm up for grabs,' he murmured.

Jessica slanted thoughtful eyes on him. 'Not all single women go to someone's wedding and immediately think that the best man is up for grabs if he happens to be single,' she returned. 'Besides, you must have lots of experience when it comes to deflecting unwanted attention...'

'Over a four-day period it could get a little trying, and at this point in time... Put it this way, I would rather steer clear of anyone in search of involvement.'

'Well, just so long as we don't have to pretend to be romantically involved...'

'Oh, we don't have to pretend anything,' Curtis refuted. 'No one is going to ask me to elaborate on our relationship and no one can doubt that we are intimately involved... That's the joy of a friendship that spans more than a decade—there's no need to work at acting relaxed in each other's company because we already are...'

Jess shivered because the last thing she felt at the moment was *relaxed* in his company, but she could see his logic.

Assumptions would be made and it would just be a case of going along with them. They had always been easy with one another and their casual familiarity would answer unasked questions. He was hardly the sort who would advertise a relationship with physical displays of affection.

There had been method in his decision to ask her to tag along.

She had a twinge of nerves as they entered the vast lodge. The door was opened by a uniformed member of staff and their names were formally taken and checked against a printed list.

Out of sight, she could hear the sound of voices and laughter, the low steady rumble of people having a good time, but she couldn't see anyone because they were all scattered in the bowels of the sprawling villa.

This was the holding pen where guests were ticked off a list because you could never be too careful. Although who on earth would want to gatecrash a fancy gathering in a ski lodge that sat in its own snowy grounds was anybody's guess. Who would dare?

'Your coats?'

As she absently removed her coat to hand to yet another member of staff who had appeared out of thin air, she was busily dealing with a sudden onset of nerves just at being somewhere where she would know absolutely no one at all and already envisaging being left to her own devices by Curtis, who would want to socialise with old friends. She decided that it would be an opportunity to brush up on her small talk skills with strangers.

Likewise, Curtis was gearing himself up for an evening of mingling. Small talk invariably ended up boring him to death, so the prospect was not an enticing one.

It was good that she had asked him about the charade about to commence, although he really didn't think it was about deceiving anyone into thinking anything, merely establishing boundary lines because John's wife-to-be was a model and there would be a bevy of models in the wings and, whatever anyone said, he would be targeted, the thought of which left him exhausted.

Surrounded by John's family and friends, it would have been an unpleasant task having to evade potential predators. That said, he had established Jess's role and emphasised the solid friendship between them. That had been a good idea, given the way his mind had strayed earlier on.

Coat dispatched, he turned to her and froze.

The sterling qualities of friendship, which he had just been mentally applauding, flew through the window faster than a speeding bullet.

His body was jump-started at supersonic speed and what he had felt only hours before when he had seen her in that ski outfit paled in comparison to what he was feeling right now.

Nothing was left to the imagination. Or rather too much was left to the imagination, and his imagination was having a field-day conjuring up all manner of forbidden images.

His hands itched to slip under the neckline of that dress to find the heavy weight of her breasts. He wondered what her nipples would look like, would taste like...

He clenched his fists and gritted his teeth and managed to step forward to politely usher her in the direction of the noise.

'You...' he said in a stifled undertone, 'you've gone the extra mile with the dress.'

'Do you like it?'

'It...it's unexpected... I don't believe... ah...that I've ever seen you in something like that...'

'A change is as good as a rest,' Jess piped up. She didn't want to look at him because she feared that she might find it hard to tear her eyes off him. Underneath the coat, he was wearing a pair of black trousers and a white shirt, with a charcoal-grey V-necked jumper in the softest cashmere. He succeeded in looking both casual and insanely elegant at the same time.

'Ah...'

When he failed to continue, she looked at him quizzically, braced to defend her choice of clothing and to stand up for statuesque women and their right to wear whatever they chose to.

'Yes?' She arched an eyebrow and he flushed.

'Nothing.' He circled her arm with his hand. 'Don't be nervous,' he added, for want of anything better to say. 'I know you don't like this kind of event.'

'I never used to,' she said airily, 'but that was years ago. I've got a lot more confident since I've been teaching. When you have to control a classful of kids and establish order, you can't afford to be too much of a shrinking violet.'

'Got it,' he muttered.

They paused ahead of the sequence of bustling rooms. It was an open-plan space that managed to retain separate areas with the clever use of partitions and banks of plants and two open fireplaces. Through the vast expanse of glass overlooking the mountains, the view was surreal in its empty whiteness.

Waiters circulated, balancing trays of food and drink.

'I thought it was going to be a little less… crowded.'

'So did I.' He shrugged. 'Don't worry. I don't plan on staying long.'

'I'm not worried,' she said irritably. About to reassure him that he was no longer dealing with the insecure girl who'd shied away from parties, she followed his gaze to where he was staring narrowly at a slight figure reaching for a glass of champagne.

'Jesus,' he swore softly under his breath. 'You're not going to believe this, but Caitlin is here...'

CHAPTER FOUR

IT TOOK A few horrified seconds for that to
sink in, even though the evidence was standing straight in front of Jess in the form of five-
foot-nothing of drop-dead gorgeous Barbie
doll in a tight, short red dress and killer heels.

She jerked Curtis off to the side, behind the
wall, and hissed, 'Did you know that your ex
was going to be here?'

Jess had met Caitlin twice, when he had
brought her to visit his godfather. Towering
over the dainty blonde, and still in her comfort-
eating phase, Jess had never felt more self-conscious, and being introduced by Curtis as *'My
best friend...don't know what I'd do without
her...'* had failed to help matters, making her
sound halfway between shrink and favourite
maiden aunt.

'I had no idea.'

'So you *didn't* invite me here as a buffer
against awkwardness from your ex...?'

'Would I be so devious? I admit,' he said grudgingly, while handfuls of people continued to walk past them towards the open area just out of sight, 'I knew a couple of girlfriends from distant times past might be on the scene, but you have my word that I had no idea that Caitlin was going to be here.'

Things fell into place abruptly. Vague stories of wanting to dodge female predators with stars in their eyes, true though that might very well have been, had probably come second to a very real desire on Curtis's part to avoid the attentions of women he had probably dumped. He was always unfailingly fair, he had once told her, telling the women he went out with that he wasn't interested in anything long-term, but did that mean all his exes relished the time when he decided that they had gone past their sell-by date? Did that mean that they all shrugged their shoulders and parted with a rueful shake of their heads and the words *That's only fair, I was warned after all* in their minds?

Doubtful.

'We can't huddle out here for much longer,' he broke the silence to say. 'Pretty soon they'll send out a search party to find out where we are. Philippa knows we've arrived. She caught my eye over the waiter with the tray of champagne cocktails.'

'I never signed up to this,' Jess all but wailed and he looked at her with sympathy.

'Nor did I,' he said grimly. 'But here we are and there's not a damn thing either of us can do about it.'

Navy eyes met green and Jess breathed in deeply because he was right, of course, here they were. And it wasn't as though she could skulk out and find the nearest taxi to deliver her back to the sanctuary of the hotel.

She reminded herself that she was twenty-six years old, a woman with a responsible job and why on earth should it matter that Caitlin was going to be around for a weekend that now seemed to stretch into infinity?

She wasn't the insecure girl who preferred to blend into the background and leave the limelight to others. She had moved on since those times.

Unfortunately, she was still paralysed with nerves as he gently eased her from where she appeared to have taken root by the side of the wall. Fear and the yearning to flee were emotions that could be recalled without warning. It was easy to be driven back to a place in the distant past and Jess made a concerted effort not to find herself returning there now because she was confronted with just the sort of petite beauty who had once made her feel so ungainly and clumsy as a self-conscious teenager. She took a deep breath and steeled herself.

This was no polite gathering. Largely a young crowd, the noise levels reflected scores of slightly tipsy people talking loudly to make themselves heard. Everyone was beautiful. In truth, Jess had never seen a collection of so many glittering peacocks gathered in one room in her life before.

She slanted a sideways glance and was momentarily startled to see something very much looking like jaded cynicism on Curtis's face, although when he turned to meet her eyes she had to wonder whether she had imagined it.

'Deep breaths.' He smiled reassuringly. 'It'll all be over in a couple of hours… Caitlin or no Caitlin…'

'I'm very happy to leave before you—' she

hoped he would take her up on the offer '—if you want to stay longer and enjoy the company. Or not as the case may be.' How would he feel about seeing his ex-fiancée? Was he as emotionally detached as he appeared to be or was that just an act? Surely he would feel *something* in the presence of the one and only woman ever to have dumped him? And a woman he had cared enough about to want to marry. Jess didn't think she could bear to see him chatting to Caitlin, reminding her of her own foolish, misplaced feelings.

Curtis killed that wild hope stone-dead. 'Perish the thought.'

And then he was leading her through the throng and she was conscious of eyes on both of them, of heads turning as they walked towards John and Philippa, their hosts. She had to resist the temptation to tug her dress down or fiddle with the neckline and at the first opportunity she managed to swipe a champagne cocktail from a passing waiter. Dutch courage.

She was introduced to the groom and his bride-to-be and to his parents and she chatted and sipped her champagne and, at one point, became quite vivacious on the subject of skiing and the slopes she longed to try. That said, her ears and eyes were vigilant for Caitlin, ever conscious of the frailty of the confidence she had meticulously built up for herself over the years.

She had expected Curtis to leave her to her own devices so that he could mingle with friends he probably didn't get a chance to see much of during the course of the year and she was surprised when instead he chose to stick to her side. Like glue.

There was no formal meal, no buffet with a rowdy queue snaking through the elegant living areas, but a constant supply of exquisite finger foods ferried through the party crowd by an army of uniformed waiters and waitresses. No glass was left unfilled for longer than five seconds.

She had almost forgotten about Caitlin, having made sure to stay put in a very small circle of people, when she heard a voice from behind and both she and Curtis turned as one to find the diminutive blonde right behind them.

Slightly the worse for wear, she tottered on her very high heels with a drink in one hand and her white blonde hair in some disarray.

Even so, the woman, Jess thought grudgingly, was beautiful. She had naturally full, pouting lips and huge pale blue eyes and very straight hair that hung in a curtain to her waist. Despite the fact that it was the very depths of winter, she had a light golden tan that spoke of expensive holidays in the tropics.

'Curtis—' she dimpled '—I wondered whether I'd see you here!' She looked up at Jess. 'How lovely of you to bring your friend from the village.'

Jess wondered how it was that she had somehow found herself reduced to village idiot status.

'Caitlin.' Jess smiled politely. 'How are you?'

'You look different.'

'Do I?'

'I'm very well. Would you mind awfully if Curtis and I had a private word together?'

'She really would.' Curtis smiled, not unkindly, and, to Jess's shock, he slipped his arm around her waist, a gesture that did not go unnoticed by the other woman, who narrowed her eyes to slits.

'I had no idea you two were an item,' she mused. 'You kept that one under your hat, didn't you?' She laughed but there was a hard, hurt edge to her laughter.

'There are aspects of my private life,' Curtis said, 'that are not for public consumption. Caitlin, it's been nice seeing you. You look well. Now, if you'll excuse us...'

'Please, Curtis, I just want to chat to you for a moment...'

Next to her, Jess could sense him stiffening. Something about the scene playing out was at odds with the reality of a woman who had been the one to do the breaking of an engagement, but Jess decided that that was none of her business. What *did* fluster her was that hand still securely circling her waist and sending her nervous system into freefall, and what *did* upset her was knowing that the only reason that hand was there was to say something to his ex.

'I should say goodbye to John's parents.' She smiled and inched away from the red-hot branding iron of his arm. They had only just been talking to them but everyone had melted away with Caitlin's arrival. Perhaps they'd all sensed a possible awkward scene in the making, although there was nothing embarrassing about their stiff exchange. No raised voices or muttered oaths or shouty recriminations. If anything, Curtis looked a little frustrated but strangely tolerant where she might have expected a little more anger and certainly a lot more reluctance to be cloistered with his ex, who had given him the boot in a very public manner over a year ago.

Before either could respond, Jess walked away, seeking out the older, amiable hosts who were chatting to a little group and instantly included her in the conversation.

If anyone thought it strange that she had left Curtis and Caitlin together whispering who knew what, no one showed the slightest curiosity.

This, she decided, was *exactly* what she needed to cure herself of her foolish infatuation with him. Seeing him in his natural habitat, pursued by his ex and surrounded by just the sort of blonde bombshells he was so accustomed to dating.

She had no idea who the past girlfriends were but, from the high number of extraordinarily good-looking women present, they could have been any of them.

This was a world where Curtis moved with ease, sophistication and self-assurance. He was one of them—at home in billion-dollar properties where helipads were *de rigueur* and jewellery was kept in bank vaults only to be worn on special occasions. He might be a self-made billionaire, unlike many there who had been born into money, but he was so self-assured, so respected and feared in that complex world where big money was made, that no one would ever have questioned his right to be there.

They were good friends because they went back a long way, but the bottom line was... she was a teacher and very far removed from this glitzy crowd.

She couldn't help glancing over to him as she made small talk with the people around her. What did he and Caitlin have to discuss? He might have been shocked and alarmed to find that she would be part of the guest entourage, but he didn't look particularly uncomfortable in her presence, so what was that all about?

Had he been so in love with the other woman that he was willing to put the past behind him and give her a second chance?

He'd certainly said absolutely nothing about

what had been behind the end of the relationship and now all sorts of questions were jump-
ing out from hiding places Jess hadn't even
known existed in her head.

Coming here might allow her to put things in
perspective insofar as she was being afforded
a glimpse of what kind of life he led and how
inappropriate he was and always would be as
a candidate for her heart because their worlds
could not have been more different but, con-
versely, it was also opening up a Pandora's
box of curiosity.

'Huh?' She blinked and realised that someone had asked her a question about the Na-
tional Curriculum and, by rote, she launched
into a conversation about Independent versus
State education.

She half turned so that Curtis and Caitlin
were no longer in her line of vision and when,
after twenty minutes, she felt hands on her
shoulders she practically leapt with surprise.

'Time to wend our weary way back,' he murmured and, to her consternation, he did more
than slide a hand across her waist as he had
earlier done. This time he bent and brushed
her neck with his mouth, a feathery kiss that

temporarily turned her to stone. The smile froze on her lips, her eyes glazed over. He then rested his hand on the nape of her neck, under her hair, and left it there. The sounds around them suddenly became background white noise, over which she swore she could hear the crashing of her heart against her rib-cage.

What the heck was going on?

This wasn't part of any scenario she had imagined! Was he playing games with her? Somehow trying to make his ex jealous? Was that it?

Her body was as heavy as lead and yet, curiously, wobbly and shaky. Every nerve in her body was alive to the thrill of his hand against her neck, absently caressing underneath her hairline. She should be angry but she was too wildly aware of his touch for any other emotion to find a way through.

She breathed slowly, steadying her nerves.

This was what came of an inappropriate crush, she agonised, while her nerves continued to fray and her body sizzled with dark, forbidden excitement.

If she could track back, she could work out

just when she'd become aware that what she felt for Curtis had morphed into a crush.

If she traced through time, and she frequently had over the past few months, she could work out that there was a point when adolescence, with all its complexities, had replaced the innocence of childhood.

Everyone in her class and at the afterschool club, all the girls, had started to change, physically and mentally. Boys had gone from annoying and stupid to riveting and worth getting dressed up for. And how her friends, who were all so much smaller and skinnier than her, had enjoyed the transition!

Yet she, Jess, had been the one to develop the fastest, shooting up in height, taller and bustier than all her friends.

And boys had stared. She could remember shying away from the attention, well aware that they hadn't been staring at *her* but at her breasts, which no school uniform could successfully conceal.

She'd become adept at covering up and maybe, she often thought, that had become a habit, a display of insecurity about her body that had lasted for years, dictating what she wore and how she interacted with the opposite sex.

When her father had died she'd turned to comfort eating and the heavier she had become, the more she had hidden herself under shapeless, baggy outfits. As a teacher, it was a manner of dressing she could get away with because comfort always trumped style.

And yet, through it all, Curtis had been there for her, from the very moment she had met him as a kid in his godfather's house, right through adolescence, with all its challenges, none of which she'd ever talked to him about because she'd been just so happy to be in his company.

Was it any wonder that she had developed an almighty crush on him over the years? Was it any wonder that, between her own insecurities and that idiotic crush, there had been no room to actually contemplate the business of getting out there and dating?

Until now…

Until she had woken up in the wake of his engagement, despite the fact that it had not led down the aisle. Until she had seen just how much of her life was being wasted in a hopeless infatuation with someone who would never look at her in *that* way. Until she had got her act together and changed her lifestyle and now, recently, started dating. Her confidence levels had risen so much in the past few months.

Unfortunately, lack of experience when it came to men was not standing her in good stead now, and she couldn't help but feel knocked back when she had looked down at the tiny blonde girl who had stolen Curtis's heart.

So how did she deal with that hand caressing the back of her neck? How did she get past her lack of experience to handle a body that had gone into meltdown? The truth was that Curtis liked the fact that she spoke back to him, that she didn't bow and scrape in an attempt to please. He liked her outspoken irreverence. What would he do were he to realise that that was only a thin veneer concealing an inherent shyness and the hangover of self-consciousness from way back when?

She surfaced to find that goodbyes had been said and she smiled and said all the right things, though her mind whirled with the confusion of knowing, at least for her, that the status quo that had existed between them was being called to account, that foundations were shaking and the comfort of knowing where things stood could no longer be relied upon.

When she looked around, it was to find, to her surprise, that the room had emptied. They weren't the first to leave. They were among the last and there was no sign of Caitlin.

They went to gather their coats, Jess having shaken his hand off, making sure to keep a healthy distance between them, but when they were in the back of the chauffeur-driven four-wheel drive she turned to him and said, with driven urgency, 'Are you going to tell me what all that was about?'

'Did you find it disconcerting?'

Had she found it disconcerting? Jess nearly guffawed with manic laughter at that question. She couldn't think when she had last been so disconcerted by anything.

'I didn't find it *disconcerting*, Curtis! I found it *bewildering*!' she denied vigorously. 'I thought there wasn't going to be any pretending that we were anything other than friends...'

'Not quite the conversation as I remember it.'

'Meaning?' For once, the spectacular panorama of white snow, dazzling despite the darkness, was lost on her as she feverishly looked at him in the semi-darkness of the car.

'Meaning we agreed that we would let our friendship do the talking. We wouldn't have to pretend anything because we would rely on assumptions being made and, since it would be perfectly clear that we're involved with one another, there would be no need for us to define the nature of the involvement.'

'Well, be that as it may—' Jess sidestepped that interjection because he was right '—you still haven't answered my question. What's going on with the bewildering gestures of affection?' Without thinking, she rubbed the back of her neck in an unconscious gesture to scrub away the feel of his touch there.

Watching her closely, expression veiled, Curtis took in that small gesture and shifted. For the first time in their long history, he had touched her in a manner that wasn't completely platonic.

Scratch that—there had been one time, the

only one, single time, when he had touched her and felt his body respond in a way that had shocked him. That kiss under the mistletoe. It was a million years ago but he must have kept the memory lodged in his head somewhere because it rushed to the forefront now, now that he was recognising that something had shifted between them. At least as far as he was concerned.

From her perspective...not so. That was the gesture of someone who had been irritated by the feel of his hand on her neck.

He could barely admit it to himself, but he had enjoyed being by her side at the party, hadn't particularly wanted to branch out because her conversation was so much more invigorating and because she demanded more conversationally from the people she was with, and they duly obliged.

When he *did* veer off to catch up with some of the guys he hadn't seen for months, he'd still found himself seeking her out, his gaze resting on her just a little too long. She'd seemed oblivious to the attention she'd been getting but he hadn't been. He'd seen the way some of the men there had glanced at her, appreciating her curves. They would never have said anything because they'd all been under the impression that she was with him but they still hadn't been able to stop what had been an automatic gesture of appreciation of her considerably sexy assets.

And when he'd touched her...

That same knee-jerk reaction he'd had at the airport when she'd whipped off the shapeless jumper to reveal a body that had stunned him into utter confusion.

'Caitlin seemed to think that for our relationship to go from good friends to lovers was open to question, and...'

He raked his fingers through his hair and fell into momentary silence until she prodded, 'And...?'

'Possibly a conversation best left until tomorrow morning.'

'Why?' Jess asked with genuine puzzlement.

'It's complicated.'

'Does it still matter what your ex thinks about you and your love life?' she demanded sharply.

After some hesitation, Curtis murmured in a low voice, 'Yes.'

* * *

One word but it was like a physical blow and Jess recoiled from it because if ever there was confirmation that he was still in love with Caitlin, then this surely was it.

As a rule, Curtis Hamilton had never cared two hoots about what people thought of him. They were entitled to their opinions was his take, but he wasn't interested in letting what they thought influence his behaviour.

He'd once told her that but, even if he hadn't, she would have guessed simply from watching how he dealt with so many situations. He had always had an inner strength that was completely undeterred by what other people thought of him or said to him.

So the fact that he was willing to alter his behaviour because of his ex said something.

'Well, maybe, Curtis, *I* may not want to play games with you and pretend that we have a relationship if that means you touching me.' She rubbed the back of her neck again, more vigorously this time, and looked at him with thinly veiled hostility. She was reminded of just how devastating that casual touch had been, throwing her senses into complete disarray and putting her on the back foot when it came to the whole business of getting him out of her system by putting him into perspective.

He stiffened. 'My apologies if you felt… uncomfortable, Jess.'

'I didn't feel uncomfortable.' She shook her head unhappily. 'I just… I know she still means a lot to you but that's no reason… What were you trying to do? Make her jealous? Was that it? By touching me?' Joining the dots, that seemed the most likely explanation and she did her best not to sound hurt and stung.

'Far from it.'

'I refuse to be involved in whatever situation there is between the two of you.' Jess was loath to let it go. Jealousy was an ugly emotion, in her eyes, yet she could feel it sinking its teeth into her, hard as she fought against it.

She'd barely noticed the scenery moving slowly past them as the car carefully wound its way to their hotel, so she was surprised when it drew to a smooth stop.

The air outside was cold and crisp and they both hurried into the warmth of the hotel. She paused, relishing the change of temperature, before turning to Curtis.

'Let's talk tomorrow,' he said before she could pick up where she had left off. 'It's late.'

Jess looked at him narrowly and he shot her just the ghost of a weary smile.

'You have a very expressive face, Jess, and right now I'm seeing doubt written all over it. You think I'm going to try and avoid the subject come morning...'

'Can you blame me?' She hoped her face wasn't quite as expressive as he seemed to think because the last thing she needed was for him to guess the effect he had on her. 'You're not exactly a guy who likes to have heart-to-heart conversations, and I guess you're sensitive on the topic of your ex, and I don't care. But I'm here now, *at your behest*, and it's only fair that you tell me what's going on.'

'At my *behest*...? Little wonder you and my godfather get along so well...' But as the lift doors closed on them he turned to her and said, utterly serious now, 'No need to fear. We'll talk tomorrow.' Then he smiled. 'Even though you're right when you say that I'm not the kind of guy who believes in tearfully pouring his emotions out.'

They were on their corridor and she reached into her clutch for the door key. She could feel his presence next to her as he leant against the wall and watched her.

'Meet me for an early breakfast,' he murmured just as she pushed open her door to stand framed by the light from behind.

'Okay.'

'We can talk and then we can ski.'

'I think there's some stuff planned…activities for bored other halves.'

'You're never bored when you're with me so that automatically excludes you.'

Jess shivered and dragged in a silent, ragged breath. Did he have any idea how intimate he could make a simple observation seem? How easy it was for him to ignite her imagination until it became a conflagration?

'What sort of activities have they lined up?'

'Trips…tours… I believe there's a wine-tasting experience…'

'Scrap them. We'll have breakfast and then we'll spend the morning on the slopes.' He glanced at his watch and straightened. 'Okay.

I'll meet you in the restaurant at…eight to-morrow morning. Or I could order room service, which might be a better idea if we want some privacy.'

'No!' Jess cleared her throat and frowned thoughtfully. 'No, the restaurant will be just fine.' She thought about sitting opposite him at the little circular table in her room, with a bed announcing itself in the background, and could think of nothing worse. 'And yes, okay, eight.' She smiled with genuine anticipation at the thought of a morning skiing. 'And then we can hit the slopes. I believe you have some catching-up to do.' It was a stilted attempt to reclaim some of that shaky ground that had suddenly opened up between them, to regain their easygoing familiarity and to forget, just for a second, that if she stared into those green eyes for too long she would feel as if she were drowning.

'Is that so?' He smiled. 'I believe I gave you quite a substantial head start but…' He shrugged and raised his eyebrows. 'If you really think you're up to proving superior skiing skills then…who am I to argue? At your behest, I'm more than willing to drop the head start...'

In treacherous waters, the absolute bliss of normality between them kept the smile on her face as she shut the door and went straight to the bathroom to have a quick shower.

She let the water run off her and for the first time, after she had towel-dried, she stood in front of the standing mirror and looked at herself.

It was not something she ever did. Ingrained in her from her much bigger days was a certain amount of ambivalence when it came to looking at herself without any clothes on.

She did now. She was tall and she was bountifully built, and she wondered whether Curtis had had to grit his teeth when he'd touched her.

She swung around, pulled on her pyjamas—which consisted of a loose, brightly patterned T-shirt and a pair of stretchy shorts that barely skimmed her thighs.

Despite the cold and snow outside, it was warm in the bedroom. And, despite the buzzing questions in her head, she fell asleep as soon as her head hit the pillow.

Her last thought was, *I wish I'd never come...*

I think... And her first thought the following morning was, *Who the heck is knocking on my door? Have I somehow forgotten to flip the Do Not Disturb sign over?*

Before the cleaners could decide to service the room while she was only just out of bed, Jess flew to the door and pulled it open sufficiently to realise that it wasn't any member of staff who had been knocking.

'What are you doing here?' She shuffled as far back behind the door as she could possibly manage and peered at a bright-eyed and bushy-tailed Curtis, dressed in black trousers for skiing and a tight black thermal, which she just about glimpsed underneath his black V-necked sweater. He hadn't bothered to shave and the stubble on his chin struck her as ferociously sexy.

She gulped, conscious of her legs on display because there was only so much concealing she could do without rudely closing the door in his face.

'Have you forgotten our breakfast date?' He looked pointedly at his watch. 'It's eight-thirty. I thought I'd knock on your door to make sure you weren't the worse for wear.'

* * *

He kept his eyes pinned to her face. She was pink and flushed and still in her nightwear. Some kind of patterned top and a pair of bottoms that left absolutely nothing to the imagination. Her legs were smooth and long and he could see the sway of her unconstrained breasts, soft and bouncy against her arms, which were across them.

She looked tousled in the sexiest way imaginable.

Hence his focus on her face. He didn't want to risk his eyes straying to more dangerous zones.

Before he could open up a dialogue on the issue of time-keeping, he decided to head back down to the restaurant because the less he saw of her in all her drowsy, ruffled glory, the better. He wasn't sure whether it was a new phenomenon, but it seemed that his prized self-control was under threat when she was around and the worst of it was that he didn't seem to mind anywhere near as much as he should…

'Doesn't matter,' he said tautly, backing away and shuffling ever so slightly before glancing in her direction again. 'How long should I be expected to hang around waiting for you to join me?'

That came out not at all as he had intended, and he noted the way she stiffened but, hell, he wasn't going to apologise because he just wanted to clear off before his imagination had a chance to take over completely.

Looking at him and hearing the curtness in his voice, Jess's voice was cool when she replied. 'Give me half an hour. Will that do, or is that too late for someone as busy as you, Curtis?'

'I'll see you there.'

CHAPTER FIVE

DESPITE BEING BUSY with the early to ski crowd, the restaurant managed to feel calm, quiet and relaxed. No crowds forming an unruly conga line by the breakfast buffet bar. Instead, there was an attractive cornucopia of fresh fruit and a selection of every cheese imaginable, with baskets of freshly baked breads and a comprehensive menu for anyone who wanted anything of the cooked variety.

Jess spotted him before he saw her and she stopped dead in her tracks, an automatic reaction to his physical beauty as he lounged in his chair, staring at whatever held him spellbound on his cell phone.

Unremitting black suited him, she thought stupidly. She took a deep breath and headed directly towards his table and smiled as their eyes briefly met.

'I must say, this is very different to my experience of breakfast in a hotel on a skiing trip with Year Eight,' she told him, sliding into her chair and watching as he straightened and looked at her.

'I imagine it is.'

Jess laughed nervously because of his thoughtful expression, so rare in someone who was essentially the very essence of light-hearted charm and teasing banter.

Wasn't this what she had secretly longed for, though? A Curtis who moved from superficial charm to offer her a glimpse of the depths that swirled underneath?

The conversation she had demanded felt inappropriate over breakfast before taking to the slopes and there was a part of her that almost wished she hadn't. She enjoyed their familiar routine, even if she was restricted by it, and this felt like a seismic shift in something that had been an anchor point in her life over the years.

'You wouldn't believe the chaos,' she gamely carried on as coffee was poured for them and the menu inspected and discarded in favour of the cold continental options, 'when you have twenty-odd kids scuffling to see who can make it to the bacon first...'

'You asked about my relationship with Caitlin...'

'It doesn't matter,' Jess said quickly.

'Doesn't it? What changed overnight?'

'As long as I don't have to pretend to be anything we're not, then I don't care what sort of relationship you have with her, or whether it's over or not.'

'It's firmly over, Jess,' he told her, pausing only to give his order to one of the serving staff. 'Why don't you go and get whatever you want from the buffet and we can talk about this when you're back. Get it out of the way.'

'Honestly, Curtis...' She leaned towards him, elbows on the table, and looked at him earnestly. 'It really doesn't matter. I don't see what the problem is if you're no longer...an item.'

'Why did you imagine that we were?'

Instead of answering that she headed for her breakfast, giving herself time to think about his question and half hoping he might forget that he had asked it at all, but as soon as she sat back down with her plate of cheese and bread in front of her he repeated it.

'I suppose that huddled conversation in the

corner of the room last night.' She shrugged and felt the bite of jealousy again but this time it was muted because she believed him when he told her that whatever relationship they had enjoyed was over. 'You looked... You didn't look like a guy who's over a woman.'

'How does a guy who's over a woman look?' he asked with genuine curiosity. He attacked his food with relish, but she could feel the focus of his laser-sharp attention firmly pinned on her, making her restless and fidgety.

'You looked as though you still cared about her,' she muttered, staring down at her plate. She cleared her throat and toyed with the bread and cheese, eyes flicking up to him every so often. 'And, to be honest,' she confessed, 'you always struck me as the sort of person who ends a relationship without any messy, unfinished strands of it left to resurface at a later date.'

Curtis's green eyes were thoughtful. 'You know me well.'

'So, if that's the case, then how is it that you're obviously still attached to Caitlin? How is it that you still care what she thinks?' Jess hoped that the jealousy she was banking down hadn't found its way into her voice, but she wasn't convinced and when she looked at him his expression was serious and unreadable.

'You wanted to know why we broke up.'

'I *know* why you broke up. It was in the gossip columns. She dumped you because she didn't think you were a long-term match. I think the implication was that you weren't enough fun for her.'

'I admit there might be some who find me a bore.' He half smiled but his eyes were serious when he spoke again. 'I have never talked to anyone about this,' he began, pushing his plate to one side and leaning towards her, his expression as grave as she had ever seen. 'Not even to William, although he wasn't as curious as I might have expected. Probably didn't want to jinx the situation by asking too many questions. Not sure he ever saw Caitlin as a match made in heaven for me.'

'Who knows?' Jess murmured vaguely.

'You, I expect.'

She blushed and inclined her head to one side but could hardly deny that wry observation.

'Caitlin and I got engaged because she told me that she was pregnant.'

His words dropped between them like a rock thrown into still water, spreading ripples outwards until the ripples absorbed everything. For a minute Jess's brain seemed to stop completely. She had never been so shocked in her life before because it was the last thing she'd expected him to say.

She knew she was staring with her mouth open, but she couldn't help herself.

'You're surprised.'

'That's putting it mildly!'

'I say she *told* me that she was pregnant. It was an elaborate lie designed to get exactly what she wanted. A marriage proposal. She showed me the evidence, the positive pregnancy test. What I didn't realise was how she got hold of it. She managed to convince someone she knew who *was* pregnant to hand over one because she wanted to play a joke on a friend.'

'I don't understand… Why on earth would she do that, Curtis? It's not as though she could carry on faking a pregnancy for nine months.'

'No, but she could fake one until we were married, only to tragically have a miscarriage. I found out because the girl she duped, someone who was far removed from her social circle, a satellite she befriended on a shoot somewhere abroad, joined the dots and came to me.'

'This is crazy.'

'I confronted Caitlin and she confessed.' He sighed, raked his fingers through his hair and looked at her. 'Caitlin has…many issues. As soon as I found out the whole shocking truth, I naturally called off the engagement but…'

'But…?

'Caitlin, as I discovered, was obsessed with me. It was something I only recognised in stages and by the time I wanted to bow out… well, it seemed to be too late. She came to me with the pregnancy story.'

'And you would have actually *married* her because she was pregnant?'

'I believe in the sanctity of family life,' he said gruffly. 'Believe it or not.'

Don't we all want the things we are denied? Especially when those things denied are rooted in our childhood?

'So… I still don't quite understand, Curtis.'

'Caitlin has…an unfortunate background.

She was pretty upset when I told her I wanted out. Felt humiliated. She mistakenly imagined that I might spread the story of the fake pregnancy. Of course, she could not have been further from the truth, but the fact is that I felt sorry for her, despite what had happened.'

'Because…she had an unfortunate background?'

'Correct.' He looked at her for one long moment, his eyes shuttered. 'I told her that she could tell the world whatever she wanted on the condition that she had therapy, which I was more than happy to pay for, for however long it took.'

So many gaps in the telling, Curtis thought, but even so he was curiously glad to be talking to Jess. It occurred to him that, whatever she thought, there would be a level of empathy at the very heart of her that would stop her from prying because there were things he had no intention of sharing.

The past, for Curtis, was a place where sadness was buried, where memories were too painful to bring out for inspection. It was a place he preferred to keep locked away because to go there would always feel too steep a mountain to climb. He might occasionally confront the darkness inside him, but he would never share it with anyone else.

He had told her that Caitlin had an unfortunate past. He would never tell her that that unfortunate past was what had kept him tethered to her even when he'd recognised that he should get out. She had been in and out of foster care most of her life and had emerged, at the age of eighteen, tough and determined to leave a miserable past behind her.

He had not been in foster care for the length of time that she had, but he had been there and could remember what fear and loneliness and abandonment had tasted like. The two years he had spent there after his mother died had made him understand what it meant to look at a future where love would be in very short supply because when he'd been put there, at the age of six, he'd been just a little too old to be desirable for adoption. Too old to adopt but not too young to care.

Those dark places he kept to himself and always would, but they had shaped him. Trust and an ability to give his heart away were commodities in short supply. He had the capacity for neither. He had formed a protective shell around himself that allowed no one in, no one but his godfather, the man who had rescued him.

Caitlin had dealt with her ordeal in another way. Her insecurities, so well hidden under that beautiful exterior, manifested themselves in a desperate need to be loved. Had she sensed something in him, some shared background, and that was why she had become so obsessive about him in such a short space of time? Obsessive enough to want him, whatever the cost? He had no idea because she certainly knew nothing about his past.

At any rate, they had broken up, but he couldn't just let her go and damn the consequences. For starters, he feared she might do something rash because she fundamentally held herself in low esteem, however deceptive appearances might have been, and a sense of responsibility also meant that he was concerned for her welfare, whatever lies she had told.

He had continued to check in on her, irregularly but enough to know that she had kept up the therapy. But he had gently held her at

arm's length when she'd begged for a recon-
ciliation. He couldn't bring himself to reject
her completely and he'd been thankful that she
had pulled back to let him get on with his life
because he would have had to reject her eventually had she not.

Seeing her the night before had been a stark
reminder that sometimes the best laid plans
did not necessarily go the predicted way.

He hadn't had contact with her for at least
three months. Despite his initial alarm when
he'd spotted her last night, he had been rea-
sonably hopeful that there would have been
no unfortunate scene.

But she had clocked the situation with Jess,
had shrewdly deduced that old friends didn't
suddenly turn into new lovers.

Had this reignited a need to have him back?
Where she had been happy enough to adhere
to his No Trespassing signs when he had dated
other women after their split, she had not been
happy when he had informed her that he and
Jess were serious about one another. Maybe
she had been simply biding her time while he
went out with other women, but Jess, someone

she knew to be an old friend, had suddenly felt more of a threat.

'I'll bet your godfather's thrilled,' she had chirped, watching him carefully. 'He didn't like me—didn't think I was good enough for you. The second time we went there, he couldn't stop talking about the girl next door. So I guess he's over the moon that you two are a serious item...'

He had set that snide observation to one side because the need to demonstrate that he wasn't up for grabs had been more important. She hadn't got over him as he'd hoped, and he was astute enough to realise that she had the potential to become obsessive, which he knew would damage her far more than it could ever damage him.

He would normally never reveal any of this, but Curtis realised that he had to share enough to explain to Jess why he had touched her that way, a first for them both. He had the weirdest sensation of having done something outrageously taboo. Worse, he had *enjoyed* it... That in itself was even more shocking to him, and it was something else he had no intention of revealing.

* * *

Jess tried to glean what he wasn't telling her but she had no idea. What he had said was so revealing and yet it raised more questions than it answered.

He was a closed book and she knew that that was probably what gave him some of the incredible authority he wielded in the world of business. He gave nothing away, and right now he was only offering her a selected sliver of a bigger picture. She didn't know why she was so sure of that, but she was.

'So, to recap,' she said slowly, dragging each and every syllable out and, for once, not at all discomfited by those green, green eyes pinned to her face, 'Caitlin is here. She's been a thorn in your side and it's a nuisance, I'm sure, that she's going to be around for the next couple of days, but I don't understand why that would pose such a problem. And I *really* don't understand why all of a sudden you had to give the impression that we really *are* an item when that was never part of the deal.'

Which neatly brought them back to square one. Curtis signalled for a refill for both of them. The beautiful room had also emptied out and she realised that time had flown past since they had begun talking.

A morning aggressively attacking the ski slopes looked to be going down the tubes.

'She doesn't buy that we have a relationship.'

'Do you really care? Does it matter if she thinks you're fair game now?' Jess was still so confused but she managed a weak grin. 'And here I was thinking that you were a big boy who wasn't scared of anything.'

Curtis burst out laughing, his eyes warm with amused appreciation. He sobered up to say, 'I mentioned Caitlin has had an unfortunate background...'

'You did.' Jess frowned. 'Why are you finding it so hard to have this conversation, Curtis?' Then, voice a shade cooler, she added, 'I realise it must be agony being a tiny bit open with me...'

'I'm more open with you than any other woman I've ever known,' he pointed out.

Jess wondered whether she was expected to take that as a compliment because on no front did it feel like one. Did he mean that he was so utterly unaware of her sexually that he found it easier to confide in her? Was she the equivalent of the hairdresser, who was confidante of many whilst being significant to none? At any rate, if he thought that he was truly open with her then he had no idea what it meant to confide, to share.

She wondered when she had started thinking this way, which made her think of Caitlin and she fixed him with a cool, silent stare.

Curtis hesitated. 'Caitlin is mentally…fragile,' he said quietly. 'I'm telling you this because I don't feel I have a choice, not at this particular moment in time. She wants to rekindle something that isn't there. I thought she was over me but, meeting her yesterday, it would seem not. She doesn't think that we could possibly be going out…'

'Why? Because we've known one another for a hundred years, or is it because of the way I look?'

'What does that mean?'

Jess shook her head and backed away from a contentious conversation at speed. 'Nothing.'

'No, talk to me. Tell me what you're trying to say.'

'I'm not tiny and blonde, Curtis. *That's* what I'm trying to say! Of course she doesn't think we're actually going out, because she doesn't believe that you could *actually* ever take an interest in me!' Raw hurt surged through her and she wanted to stand up and walk away but that would have been giving away too much, would have shown him just how much of an effect he had on her.

'Maybe,' he mused, 'she doesn't *want* to believe it.' He sounded a little surprised, as though this was a thought that was only now occurring to him. 'Maybe,' he continued, thinking aloud, going with the flow, 'she was never threatened by the women who came after her but with you…' He looked at Jess narrowly and she flushed. 'Yes, we're old friends…but you're smart, you're witty and you're sexy. Maybe she sees *you* as the threat she doesn't want to face. At any rate, whatever the reason, this weekend should be all about John and Philippa. The last thing I need is for Caitlin to dominate proceedings by trying to commandeer me, and she's unpredictable enough to not care how much of a disruption she causes.' He paused. 'I'm not sure what I would have done had John forewarned me of her presence on the scene but I'm guessing it never occurred to him that it might be a problem. He knows that I don't harbour grudges, and am pretty comfortable meeting women I've dated in the past. Either that or he wanted my presence and so diplomatically decided not to raise the subject.' He grinned. 'I'm inclined to believe the latter. A hedge fund analyst knows how to gamble for the desired outcome...'

Jess's brain had stopped whirring at that word, *sexy.* Had he actually described her as *sexy?*

Suddenly the atmosphere felt close and claustrophobic and the recollection of his hand on the nape of her neck was imbued with all sorts of different, more dangerous connotations.

Had he found her sexy when he'd been stroking the nape of her neck...? Touching her in a way he had never done before?

'I'm glad you explained.' She shot him a one-hundred-watt smile and began rising to her feet. 'I guess, all in all, we'll only be in public when we're at the wedding...and you're right, it would be awful if John and Philippa's big day was clouded by...er...antics from your ex-fiancée...'

She was keen to get skiing, disconcerted by

the way the familiar had veered off into the unknown, by the inroads being made into safe territory. 'I guess a few fond shows of affection aren't going to hurt anyone!' she trilled with nervous enthusiasm. 'And now we've gone through all that, shall we head for the slopes?'

Curtis watched as Jess tugged off the black and red striped woolly hat, releasing her hair before running her fingers through it.

Where before her body language had been that of someone trying to disappear into the background, now she was looser, more confident in her sexiness. Was it any wonder Caitlin was now so unnerved by what she must consider a real threat to any chance of them getting back together?

He had had over a dozen texts since they had chatted the evening before. He had answered one and that was to tell her that he didn't want her texting him.

It was true that he had once worried, and still did, about the fragile state of her mental health, which had encouraged her unhealthy obsession with him. He was now concerned about her unpredictability. Her texts had been intrusive and out of order. She had reverted to pleading that he give them another chance because she had changed, because the therapy had done her a world of good.

She couldn't believe he could possibly be interested in someone like Jess. Didn't he remember the fun they used to have in bed?

Curtis was seriously considering telling John that the situation was too flammable for him to stay for the wedding, although there was no part of him that didn't curse the fact that this was a situation that should never have come about in the first place.

Who was it who said that a good deed never went unpunished? He would have been better off walking away from the woman instead of trying to lend a helping hand.

The scars he carried from his own childhood had coloured his responses to Caitlin, had, for the first time in his life, blinded him to the hard-line path he had forged for himself, one from which he never wavered.

Just went to show what happened the minute you opened that door a crack and allowed emotions to start calling the shots, even in the smallest possible way.

Only William would ever lay claim to his emotions...

For once, he fully allowed the past to intrude, without the mental censoring he usually employed. He played in his head, like a movie set to warp speed, the events that had led to him being rescued from the loneliness of life in foster care. William had shown up, just like that—'a visitor' to see him. Curtis could remember sitting in that chair, feet barely touching the ground, and looking across at a kindly man he had never seen in his life before. He remembered being asked to stay where he was while Mrs Evans, the middle-aged lady in charge, who ruled the place with a rod of steel, disappeared for what had felt like ages with the kindly faced stranger.

Then she'd returned and his life had changed course for ever.

Later, in drips, he had discovered what had led his godfather to the doors of that foster care home.

William had been his mother's tutor at university, a caring guy who had done his best to keep her on the straight and narrow, and for a while, after his mother had graduated with a first-class degree, they had kept in touch. But Sophie Hamilton, herself the product of a broken home, without any support network in terms of family, had always hovered on the fringes of a bad crowd. Beautiful, clever and utterly irresponsible, she had dumped her job and vanished with Curtis and her boyfriend of the day to the world of alcohol and drugs.

She and William had parted with angry words exchanged and, soon after, his godfather had, himself, been offered a job abroad. He'd tried his best to keep in touch, he'd later told Curtis, but to no avail. From the other side of the world, he had been able only to pray and hope for the best.

Time had passed and it was only when he'd been returning to the UK, and with a new-found knowledge of all those search engines that enabled people to reconnect with old friends and acquaintances, that he'd laboriously and piece by piece found out what had happened to Sophie and his godson.

Appalled, he had descended on the fos-

ter home with rescue in mind and the rest...
history.

Yes, his godfather would have the love and
trust he denied the rest of the world. Caitlin?
A mistake and that lapse in his strict code of
behaviour? Also a mistake. Look where it had
got him.

'Hello? Where are you?'

Curtis blinked to find that his torrent of
thoughts had swept him away and now here
was Jess, standing in front of him, smiling,
her deep blue eyes curious.

And, just for a split second, he wanted to
pull her inside and sit her down and fill in all
those bits he had earlier left out, fill her in on
the dark motivations that drove him forward
and the past that had propelled him into taking
his eye off the ball, so that Caitlin, instead of
being relegated to the past, was still, unfortunately and despite his best efforts, very much
in the present.

Where had that weak compulsion come
from? he wondered, confused. Jess was his
friend and sure, he was open with her, but
confiding his innermost thoughts? He did that
with no one. So how was it that suddenly he'd

been tempted…? How was it that he looked at her and his self-control felt precarious?

'Thinking that you ski like a pro.'

He grinned and shook himself free from his thoughts. Life was something over which he needed to exert control and it paid to know the parameters of his friendship with Jess. 'But I still managed to beat you, despite the extremely generous head start…'

Had he really been thinking that…?

Jess could swear that he'd been a million miles away. Where? Work? With his wretched ex?

She hadn't had such fun on the slopes since for ever. She had set their conversation to one side and out there, racing with the cold air against her face and the wide-open white wonderland all around her, she had felt completely free.

'I don't think anyone could call two metres a "head start."' But she was laughing as they headed inside the hotel, where various employees rushed to assist them in shedding coats and ski boots. 'And who's to say I didn't *let* you win? Hmm?' She had half turned to look at him. She almost felt that she'd imagined that pensive expression on his face moments before because he was back to normal now, grinning, eyebrows raised.

'I mean,' she teased huskily, one hundred per cent of her straining towards him, caught in the moment, '*everyone* knows that men enjoy thinking that they can win at everything, including skiing down black runs...'

'Is that a fact...?'

He glanced to one side, moving those green eyes away from hers just for a moment.

She felt breathless, wired. He'd never looked sexier than when he'd been hurtling down that steep gradient slope just ahead of her, every muscle in his body ultra-confident in his own abilities. She could come close to catching him because she was such a proficient skier, but he would always outpace her.

This was what having fun felt like. She could go on dates with guys who all sounded perfectly suitable and were perfectly nice, but Curtis Hamilton was top of the leader board when it came to fun and excitement and making her heart beat so fast it felt as if it could burst out of her ribcage.

And now, as he turned to look at her, eyes boring into her until she felt heady and even more breathless, she felt his intense focus and purpose like the feathery brush of a finger against her skin.

He was going to kiss her. She knew it. She saw the way his breathing changed and the way his eyes darkened and when he lowered his head she was, oh, so ready for him.

She inched closer and arched up and the cool of his lips against hers was like nectar. Without having to think about it, she reached up and clasped her fingers together behind his neck, pulling him towards her. His tongue slid against hers and he shifted, bringing their bodies closer, deepening his kiss.

There was no one else around them. The entire world had disappeared, leaving just the two of them, immersed in a never-ending kiss.

It was rudely interrupted by a woman's voice. Even so, it took a few seconds for Jess to register Caitlin's presence next to them and it was with reluctance that she flattened her hands against his chest and took a shaky step back.

Several things came together in her head in

the space of time it took to break away from that devastating kiss and turn to a manifestly upset Caitlin.

The first was that he had obviously seen the other woman to the side and had engineered a kiss because that was what they had agreed… Keep up a show so that no ugly scenes with a volatile ex spoiled what should be the happiest day of John and Philippa's life.

And so he had kissed her.

But the second thing to enter her head was that she had kissed him back with every ounce of pent-up passion and desire inside her. She had thrown herself into that kiss as though her life depended on it and what, exactly, had been the message she had sent to him?

Definitely not the message that she was reluctantly resigned to having to display some kind of physical show of affection for the sake of appearances, lest his ex ruin the fun with her antics.

In a daze, she took a back seat while Curtis, polite to a fault, had a hushed and rapid conversation with Caitlin and then managed to steer her towards the grand front door, where a barely visible nod to one of the uniformed men on duty had the desirable effect and she was politely but firmly escorted out of the hotel and into whatever taxi happened to be waiting outside.

Jess had barely taken in a word of what had been said between them.

'I can't deal with this, Curtis.'

His eyes were still dark, still slumberous, still burning with what felt very much like real desire as they rested on her, but Jess wasn't going to fall prey to any illusions on that score. She'd made enough of a fool of herself already.

'You won't have to,' he told her huskily. 'She won't be around for the wedding.'

CHAPTER SIX

THIRTY-SIX HOURS OF unremitting battle against temptation, Curtis thought.

He'd managed to ensure Caitlin disappeared back to the UK, suitable excuses made to the host and hostess. No fuss, nothing to see here, a discreet exit, leaving the bride and groom-to-be free to enjoy their nuptials without asking any awkward questions or thinking, in any way, that her departure had anything to do with them at all.

Having sleepwalked into an engagement with her on the back of an outrageous and unforgivable lie, he had gone against all better judgement to keep open some lines of communication because he'd felt sorry for her, because, in a strange way, he'd understood.

But enough was enough.

He'd been chilled to the bone by the very real prospect of being stalked and, worse, for Jess to suffer the fallout because of him, because he'd been loose in his dealings with his ex.

'You need more intensive therapy,' he had told her coldly, *'and that will mean a residential facility. I will foot the bill, however long it takes, but you need to get your life back on track and eliminate me from it. Sadly, should you not do so...'*

Had there been any need to go into details? Not really. He wielded great power and that power stretched into all sorts of circles, ones that could impact her in a great many ways, and he had tabulated a few of them for her. He had seen comprehension dawning in her eyes.

She had a job for starters, thanks to him. A nine-to-five job, he had reckoned in the wake of their breakup, would confer a certain amount of stability and open her eyes to the process of co-operation and working with different people. She'd been in fashion, and fashion editing had been right up her street.

Would that job still be hers if she continued to plague him, to delude herself that they could ever get back together? Possibly not. Or possibly she could be transferred. The magazine was global. Life on the other side of the world would be quite different, she would find, and maybe not to her liking.

Who knew?

He had suggested an emergency of an unknown nature, too private to share, might be an excellent excuse for her hasty and premature departure from Courchevel. He was quite certain John and Philippa would understand.

In the end, he had thought, life was all about survival. He had learnt that from a young age. An irresponsible and drug-dependent parent and a couple of years in foster care, at the mercy of strangers, was a terrific lesson in instilling toughness and if he had wavered for a brief window in time, he was determined not to do so any longer.

Caitlin had read his message loud and clear. Her time was up. She'd left on the first flight back and there had been no further need for any public displays of affection.

'So you can relax,' he had informed Jess, and he'd raised both hands in a gesture of amused mock surrender as she had breathed an audible sigh of relief and smiled.

Since then…? The battle against temptation. He wanted to touch her. He wanted to touch her when they were away from public scrutiny and he wanted to touch her when they were in the presence of other people and he didn't really care who those other people were.

It all went against the grain. He had never been the kind of guy who liked public displays of affection. His friends were well aware of that, which was why Jess, as his plus one, had been such a good idea. Their 'relationship' would require no physical proof.

But he hadn't banked on her getting under his skin in all sorts of ways he would never have dreamt possible.

The more he itched to touch her, the greater his realisation that it would be a sign of weakness to do so. Worse was the fact that Jess wasn't one of his hot blondes with a sell-by date. He cared about her sufficiently to know that if he ever hurt her, he would never forgive himself. He was incapable of love and would never be willing to try and Jess was a woman who would never want anything less than a proper relationship.

So he fought the urge.

And he was aided by the fact that the attraction did not seem to be mutual. Zero. Zilch.

Aside from that one kiss when he had spotted Caitlin. Then he had kissed her and she had given herself utterly to that kiss, had moved her body against his until he had lost sight of the fact that they should have been kissing for effect only.

But since then she had returned to that comfortable place where they were great friends. Unfortunately, that place was one he no longer had much interest in occupying, even if it made sense.

Waiting for her now so that they could get to the venue for the wedding, his mind was a million miles away, playing with imagery he wanted to banish but couldn't.

Had he learnt *nothing* from his bruising experience with Caitlin? Hadn't it hit home that letting any form of emotion take precedence over common sense was something to be avoided at all costs?

Evidently not because his body was calling the shots and it infuriated him.

In the midst of his mental meanderings, he was only alerted to the fact that Jess had appeared because the noise levels of the people around him seemed to fade for a few seconds and then he raised his head, focused and saw her…

He'd thought that seeing her in that dress the other night, sexy as hell, couldn't be topped when it came to being knocked for six. He'd been wrong.

She was wearing a long red velvet figure-hugging dress that had a sufficiently dipped neckline to reveal the shadow of a bountiful cleavage. The dress was sleeveless, and a cream faux fur wrap was casually draped over her shoulders.

And the shoes… High enough for her to be on eye level with him and certainly to tower over every other woman in the vicinity.

Curtis took deep breaths and forced a smile on his face as he moved towards her.

'You look…'

'Incredible?' Jess laughed and looked up at him. Did she sound normal? She hoped so. She'd spent the past day and a half trying to appear very normal. Everything back on solid ground! Friends as they always had been! No more nonsense, having to pretend to be in a phoney relationship!

Caitlin had disappeared. She had no idea what Curtis had said to her but, whatever he'd said, it had worked.

She should have been sagging with relief that she would no longer have to put her weakness for him to the test, would no longer have to endure the dangerous racing of her pulse whenever he casually touched her to keep up appearances.

That kiss she had decided to conveniently shove to the back of her mind. He hadn't said anything since and there was no way she had any intention of raising the subject.

But it had been a heroic feat of willpower, trying to reveal nothing for the past day and a half and to be jolly and affectionate, the way she always had been, whilst being acutely conscious of the fact that lines had been breached whether she wanted to face it or not.

Lines had been breached...and words had been uttered that couldn't be taken back.

He'd said that he found her sexy...

Just recalling the words wreaked havoc with her attempt at self-control.

The laughter tapered off at the smouldering heat in his eyes as he looked at her. Her body tingled all over and she was conscious of her nipples pushing against the velvet dress, because she wasn't wearing a bra, conscious of a spreading wetness between her legs. She stumbled back a couple of inches, breathing jerkily but unable to tear her eyes away from his face.

'We should go,' she said roughly, and he nodded but he didn't move for a few seconds and then, when he did, it was without his usual easy grace.

He looked so beautiful, so breathtaking, in formal attire, white shirt, black jacket, black trousers, a uniform that should have made him look average but somehow did the opposite.

His face was darkly flushed, and she could almost breathe in the heady scent of desire.

He'd been so much his usual self ever since he had kissed her that she had convinced herself that what he felt was very distant from what she did.

Now she knew that they were on the same page when it came to *wanting*.

What did she do with that information…? Someone more experienced would not have hesitated to take advantage of it. She was crazy about the guy, for better or for worse. It was only natural that she might want to…have her first experience with him.

The mere thought of that, however, was enough to bring her out in a cold sweat because alongside that resided sheer panic and the horror of knowing that he would probably be either alarmed or amused or both by the fact that she was still a virgin.

But the dangerous thought tingled inside her as they made their way to the wedding venue.

The ceremony was moving, with only a handful of people to witness the exchange of vows in the small church. Then a battalion of white cars delivered everyone back to the chalet, which was a winter wonderland inside. Huge trailing garlands of white flowers formed lacy patterns from the ceilings, as delicate as spun silk, and urns of white orchids worked as partitions ensuring that the huge spaces were broken into smaller components.

There were lots more people attending the actual reception than had been there for the more intimate gathering where Jess had first laid eyes on Caitlin.

She should have been nervous because this

was just the sort of event nothing in her entire life could have prepared her for, but she wasn't.

Champagne flowed and the food was delicious. She drifted from group to group, keenly aware of Curtis, who never seemed to stray too far from her side.

In truth, she barely noticed the noise and the laughter and the stunning scenery outside, matched only by the stunning décor inside. At one point she drifted across to the vast bank of windows that gave out over a scene of limitless snowy mountains and behind her was Curtis's reflection. He raised a glass to her and she smiled without turning around.

Her heart was pounding when, several hours later, they found themselves saying their goodbyes to the couple. She was so conscious of Curtis slightly behind her, his body so close that she could feel the heat radiating from him, that she could barely focus on what Philippa was saying. Something about being the only bride to have her honeymoon exactly where she happened to have married because they would be skiing for the next week. She was rolling her eyes and laughing and constantly looking at her new husband with love and tenderness while he reminded her that the Maldives awaited them in four weeks' time.

Jess slipped off her shoes once in the back of the car. She wasn't looking at him, instead choosing to stare at her fingers interlinked on her lap.

'You were pretty amazing tonight.' Curtis broke the silence, his lazy eyes clocking the way she was making a big effort not to look at him when he knew she badly wanted to.

God, he had never before spent an evening in a state of such heightened anticipation.

When he hadn't been right there next to her, he'd been following her with his eyes, noting her every movement, the sexy swing of her hips as she moved through the room, her natural warmth as she chatted to various people and her endearing lack of awareness of the looks she was attracting from every guy at the reception.

He'd felt the sizzle of red-hot chemistry between them even when she wasn't looking at him and now, sitting in the back of this car, he was wired.

'Thank you,' Jess murmured.

He shifted, then reached out and placed his finger on her chin, gently turning her to face him. Then he let that finger trail a devastating path to outline her lips. She sucked in a sharp, jagged breath but she couldn't tear her eyes away from his face and, tellingly, she didn't slap his hand away.

'I couldn't take my eyes off you.'

'You…shouldn't be saying these things,' Jess whispered. 'How much have you had to drink?'

'Next to nothing, and why shouldn't I be saying these things…?' He knew. Of course he did. And she was right. But the devil was in the detail and he couldn't help himself.

'Because…' Her voice trailed off.

'Because we've always been friends?'

Jess nodded and breathed a silent sigh of relief as their hotel came into illuminated view because there was so much going on in her head that she couldn't think straight.

It was cold outside but she was on fire, itching to get out of the car, suffocating from the force of his personality and the intimacy of him so close to her. He was no longer touching her, but he might as well have been.

Amid the flurry of being escorted into the hotel by one of the ever-present uniformed staff who seemed to operate a round-the-clock service specifically to welcome guests, whatever the time of day or night, there was a brief respite.

But her thoughts continued to swirl and her pulse was still racing as, minutes later, the lift doors closed on them. Surrounded by mirrored walls, there was no escaping him. Their eyes met and there was a challenge in his that made her burn from her toes up to her hairline.

Flustered, she practically leapt out of the lift, pulling her wrap tightly around her in an unconscious effort to ward off the heated responses of her disobedient body.

She hit the door to her suite at a rapid pace and fumbled with her key card—then froze when his hand covered hers.

'Want to talk about what's going on here?' he asked softly, and Jess reluctantly gave up her frantic efforts to flee and turned to him.

'Nothing is going on.'

'We both know that's a lie.'

'So we're…' she looked at him a little despairingly and made a sweeping gesture '…out of our regular comfort zone. I guess if it feels as though… I mean…'

'Want to have this conversation somewhere that's not in the middle of a corridor?' He nodded to her room behind her.

'No, not at all.'

'Are you scared to?'

'No!'

'Okay.' He shrugged and began to turn away. 'I'm happy to pretend that none of this is going on and that this conversation never happened. We're heading back the day after tomorrow and we can return to the safety of our comfort zones.'

'No, wait…' She reached forward, one hand on his arm. In an instant, she recognised that she was at a turning point. She'd been infatuated with him for so long…

If he walked away now then yes, they would return to their comfort zones, except would it be quite as comfortable?

And would it cure her of her foolish infatuation?

If he walked away he would never look

back, and their friendship would slowly dwindle away under the weight of something that hadn't been dealt with.

Was this business that had to be finished?

Sleep with him, she thought, and she would slay the beast. She would get him out of her system once and for all. She had never gone through this process of giving herself to someone, had never wrestled with the doubts and hesitations and excitement and dread that other girls dealt with when they took those tentative steps with the first guy they slept with. Untouched, she had locked herself away in an ivory tower from which she could watch and fantasise without having to risk anything. She had hidden behind her insecurities, vaguely assuming that she would never have to put them to the test because there was no way a guy like Curtis would ever look at her.

She had presumed that she would get over him and lower her sights when it came to having an actual relationship with someone suitable. Someone suitable would not have been such a nerve-racking experience. Someone suitable would not have been six foot something of hard, honed alpha male who could make her laugh out loud and give her pause for thought, all in the space of five seconds. But here they were and the time for risk was with them. Still, her heart was thudding and her mouth was dry as she searched for a way of saying what she wanted to say, what she felt *driven* to say...

'I'm listening,' he prompted softly.

'I admit that I might be attracted to you.' She stumbled over her words and he inclined his head to one side and gazed at her. It was fallacy that tall men felt protective with women who were shorter, smaller. Watching the hectic colour in her cheeks, he felt a sudden surge of protectiveness towards this woman who had been his friend for so many years.

He was so used to women who were adept at playing the courting game. His heart twisted as she nervously tucked a strand of hair behind her ear and looked away.

His heart was not a commodity he could ever give away, but she knew that. Not just because he'd told her, but because she knew him so well, knew his history with women. They were simply two adults acting on a physical attraction neither had factored into their comfortable relationship. If they slept together, they would be doing so with their eyes wide open.

He reached out and linked his fingers through hers and ushered her the few steps to his own suite and, once inside, he dimmed the lights and led her towards the bedroom.

'I've spent all weekend wanting this,' he said roughly, turning to place his hands on her shoulders and stroking the nape of her neck. 'Relax.' He smiled. 'I know we're friends and, believe me, this is not what I was expecting, but sometimes surprises can lurk round the least expected corners...' He kissed the side of her mouth and flicked his tongue over her lips.

Jess froze. Her body wanted to respond, and her head was telling her to just go with the flow, but deep-rooted panic was trumping everything and she gulped.

'What's the matter?' he murmured as he began to unbutton his shirt. His coat and jacket had been disposed of earlier. She hadn't even noticed but, in fairness, the earth could have moved under her feet and she probably wouldn't have noticed.

'I don't know… I'm not sure…'

He stilled, banking down the surging ache between his legs. 'It's an unusual situation—I get that, Jess. I want you but you know you have every right to change your mind and walk away…'

'No, it's not that,' she said in a stricken voice.

'Then what?' Just talking felt like a feat of endurance when he wanted to do so much more.

'I'm not that experienced,' she muttered.

Curtis smiled reassuringly, oddly pleased at her honesty. He carried on unbuttoning the shirt until she could see his chest, broad and muscled. He shrugged off the shirt and she felt faint. 'I am experienced enough for both of us,' he murmured softly.

He rested his hand on his trouser zip and reached with the other hand to tug her towards him.

This time his kiss was one hundred per cent no-holds-barred *hungry.* He slid his tongue between her lips, tilting her back, plundering her mouth until she was whimpering and clinging to him, restricted in the dress and desperate to get rid of it.

He edged her towards the bed and she felt the edge of the mattress hit her knees. She almost teetered onto it.

Her arms were looped over his shoulders, her breasts pushing against his bare chest, and she moaned when he reached to unzip her dress until it was sagging open.

'No bra.' He nipped the side of her neck and she shivered and sighed, eyelids fluttering. 'I like that. Very much.'

'I'm not as slight... I'm a big girl...'

'Something else I like. Also very much.' He swept down the straps almost before she could protest or take evasive action or even shield herself from his gaze because he took her hands in his and stepped back and looked at her.

Jess closed her eyes tightly. So desperately did she want to cover herself that it took a superhuman effort not to yank her hands free of his loose hold and put them strategically in front of her.

'You're beautiful,' he murmured huskily.

At that, she sneaked a glance at him and their eyes met, his blazing with desire, hers tentative. With hesitation, she touched his chest and then stroked it, marvelling at how hard it was and loving the way he sucked his breath in as she caressed him.

He caught her hand and growled that she would have to watch out because too much excitement would make an experience he wanted to last, finish in way too short a time.

'Let me see the rest of you,' he commanded gruffly.

He slid his hands down her sides, along her waist, and pushed the dress so that it slipped further down. Jess inhaled deeply and shimmied out of it. Should she tell him that by *'not that experienced'* she actually meant *completely green behind the ears*?

No. She couldn't face his reaction. There was no reason for him to know, was there?

She stepped out of the heels, instantly losing five inches in height. Her underwear was practical cotton, nothing skimpy, and definitely no thong.

* * *

'You have a body fashioned to drive a man wild,' Curtis told her with searing honesty. 'Feel for yourself...'

He stepped towards her and in one easy motion took her hand and placed it on his prominent bulge. This was what he wanted. This was what they *both* wanted. They were two adults and if their situation was more complex than those he was accustomed to then all that was needed for clarity was for him to strip it back to the bare bones.

Mutual physical attraction.

Irresistible and overwhelming.

He killed the questions tugging at his conscience. He had spent a lifetime controlling his own destiny and if now there was a moment of vague unease that destiny might be controlling *him*, then he was quite certain that it would be a momentary blip, easily remedied in the cold light of day.

His deep affection for the woman who just happened to be turning him on to a degree that was unimaginable would not pose a problem. *She knew him better than anyone. Knew of his aversion to the sort of commitment that led to a walk down the aisle. He had explained about Caitlin...so there were no illusions waiting to be shattered.*

There was no risk to him. His heart was protected, as icy cold when it came to the murky waters of emotional involvement as the frozen tundra wastelands. It was the way he was built—the way life had moulded him. He had no illusions that could be shattered.

They were *both* going into this with their eyes wide open. Had that not been the case, then he was sure they wouldn't be here now, however hot the fire was that burned between them.

He would never—*never* risk hurting this woman and on that thought he promptly closed his mind and allowed physicality to consume his head space.

Jess's mouth went dry. She looked down and inserted her finger under the waistband of his trousers but honestly lacked the courage to actually yank down the zip. It felt surreal. Being here, being with him, having her fantasies roar into life without much warning. She wished she had the experience to handle the situation, to deal with what was happening without feeling utterly out of her depth.

'It's a little weird,' he whispered into her ear. 'I know. I get it. I understand.' He unzipped himself, stepped back and out of the trousers, eyes firmly glued to her face, and then out of the boxers.

Utterly at ease with his nakedness, he stood there in front of her and Jess gaped.

She forgot that she was clad only in her knickers. She forgot her nerves and the bloom of panic rising inside her. She forgot everything as she stared at him, so stunning in his nudity, his body a work of art. Broad shoulders and a broad chest tapered to lean hips and long muscular legs. He was a tall man and beautifully built, with the honed perfection of an athlete.

She stared at his manhood, impressively big, and almost passed out when he absently took it in his hand for a few seconds.

A little weird didn't come close to the heightened anticipation and burning confusion sweeping over her but nothing could deter her now. She was so turned on her mind was cloudy.

'Think you can handle a little bit of weird, Jess?' he murmured with a smile in his voice and he didn't give her time to answer. He kissed her and his hands were not innocently exploring now but cupping her breasts and he groaned and moved against her so that she could feel the hardness of his erection pushing against her belly. 'I love the fact that you're so tall.' His voice was thick and uneven as he rolled his thumbs over her nipples.

Jess grunted a reply, but she had no idea what she might have said because, for the first time in her life, she was *feeling*. Her body was alive with sensations, her nipples sending messages straight to that place between her legs which throbbed and ached to be touched.

She squirmed and rubbed her legs together, felt the wetness soaking her underwear.

As if reading her mind, and definitely reading whatever signals her body was giving off, he eased the underwear down too fast for modesty to provide a stumbling block.

He cupped her between her thighs with one hand and Jess froze in shock, but he was still kissing her, her mouth, her face, her neck, while that hand…

That hand moved rhythmically between her legs, slipped into the wet crease to stroke, finding her core and rubbing until she could barely breathe because her rising excitement was so intense.

She wanted to come so badly.

He edged them towards the bed and she gratefully sank onto the mattress and had a few seconds of breathing space, during which she watched as he checked his wallet for something. Protection. Of course.

Through the haze of pure lust filtered the recognition that the last thing he would want, after the fiasco with Caitlin, was an accidental pregnancy.

She was too overwhelmed to follow that thought anywhere useful. Instead, she half closed her eyes and gasped as he sank onto the bed to begin a slow, leisurely and methodical exploration of her breasts, nuzzling and sucking and caressing and driving her crazy. She arched back and groaned as he suckled, massaging them between his big hands. The abrasive rubbing of his thumbs on her sensitised nipples and the lash of his tongue against the tightened buds was beyond erotic.

She laced her fingers through his hair and arched back and writhed under the explosion of sensation. Her legs dropped open and she watched in fascinated trepidation as he trailed a path along her stomach, circling her belly button on the way, eventually finding what he was looking for, the damp mound between her thighs.

He buried his head there and Jess squirmed, embarrassed at such intimacy but then enjoying it way too much to wriggle free of that questing tongue.

She scarcely recognised her guttural moans and only felt a stab of real apprehension when he levered himself up to don protection, taking a lot longer than expected because his hands were so unsteady.

She noted all that and knew that that was the biggest compliment he could have paid her. He was as out of control as she was and that said a lot for a guy who was always in control.

He sank into her and she stiffened instantly. She'd thought she would be able to hide her lack of experience, but she'd been an idiot.

That first deep thrust had been a shock, had *hurt*, and she had reacted accordingly. Just for a split second but long enough for him to immediately pull out and when she looked at him there was raw shock on his face.

'Jess...'

'Don't talk,' she pleaded huskily.

'You're a virgin!'

Mortification seared her and she felt the prick of tears stinging the back of her eyes. She looked away quickly, but he gently turned her face so that she had no option but to look at him.

'Don't cry,' he whispered.

'I'm not,' she answered quickly and fiercely. 'So what if I'm a virgin? I want this. So stop talking and just...*do*...'

'I don't want to hurt you...' Curtis sounded as if he was talking about more than just whatever physical discomfort she might feel at having him inside her.

'You won't—' the fierceness was still in her voice but she stroked his face '—you won't hurt me, Curtis. So...please... I want this so much...want you to make love to me... No more questions...please...'

He did, a little clumsily at first and then gently, easing his way in, taking his time, sending her into orbit until she was the one calling the shots, at which point he moved faster, thrusting deeper, filling her and taking her with him, all the way to a place she'd never dreamt possible, where she shattered into a million glorious pieces.

She clung shamelessly, hooking her legs around his back and feeling him as he came inside her and then another clumsy fumble, cursing softly as he disposed of the condom.

'I'm never like this,' he said gruffly, turning her so that they were lying on their sides, facing one another, with her leg between his thighs and his over hers. Their bodies fitted so perfectly together.

'Like what?' She snuggled into him. She felt whole, complete and, yes, she knew that this was just going to be a moment in time, but she wanted to appreciate the absolute pleasure of lying in a bed with Curtis.

'I could barely control myself. That damn condom…think it slipped a bit… Damn…' But already the passing concern was wiped out by a wave of dizzying passion.

'What?' She nuzzled his neck and he reacted by clasping his hands on her buttocks so that he could pull her closer to him.

'No matter. You could have told me, Jess.'

'Why would I have done that?' She looked at him, her expression serious. She wasn't going to be coy and pretend that she didn't know what he was talking about.

'I would have been gentler...the whole way through. I'm sorry if... I didn't know, didn't suspect.'

'You were...perfect,' she said roughly, and he smiled and pushed some of her hair off her forehead.

'So were you.'

'Mutual admiration society.' She blushed and smiled and looked away. 'Who'd have thought?' When she thought about actually lying in bed with him, both of them naked, she felt the thrill of the forbidden. Never had anything tasted sweeter.

'Who indeed.' He hesitated. 'We're here for another day and a half...'

'We are.'

'Jess, I never thought...this didn't cross my

radar. No,' he mused, 'maybe it did but us… here…lovers…it wasn't a scenario I predicted.'

'Do you regret what just happened, Curtis?' she asked quietly.

She only realised how tense she had been awaiting his response when he said with a smile, 'Far from it.' He curled one finger through her hair. 'Still feel weird about this?'

She shrugged. *Yes and no*, she wanted to say. 'I might in the morning,' she admitted honestly. 'But things will return to normal.'

'I still want you,' he said bluntly. 'I don't want this to be the first and last time we sleep together.'

'What do you mean?' She felt a burst of pleasure and dared to let her thoughts travel down roads she knew were out of bounds, roads that might lead to a proper relationship. Hope bloomed against better judgement.

'Think about it,' he mused, still playing with that strand of hair, his eyes pensive. 'We've opened a door. If we walk away now, there's a risk that the door will remain open and, if it does, nothing between us will be the same again. We have to see this through to the finish line. That's my opinion. We do that and we will have history between us, but we won't be living with the notion that there's unfinished business festering somewhere, waiting to be dealt with.'

Jess thought that part of the reason she had come here had been to kill the infatuation that had had her in its grip for as long as she could remember. See him in his natural habitat and the chasm between them would snuff out inappropriate feelings. She hadn't banked on this! But was he right? Was this something that needed to be put to bed, literally and figuratively? Lest it fester and remain the unfinished business that would lay waste all her hopes for moving on with someone else?

And who knew...? a treacherous little voice suggested. *Who knew what lay down the road...? From friends to lovers... A road unexplored...possibilities born...*

'You know me better than anyone,' he continued as she chewed over what he had just said. 'You know that I'm not looking for anything long-term. We can be lovers without the worry that you might want more than what's on the table...don't you agree?'

His words hit her like a bucket of cold water, killing dead those treacherous shoots of hope.

The tableau in front of her was now somewhat different. In it, she saw herself continuing with what they had, handing her heart over to him and then, when her sell-by date came, he would politely discard her as he had discarded so many women in the past, as he would have discarded Caitlin had events played out differently.

And she would have no one but herself to blame because he would have given her ample warning that he wasn't in it for the long haul.

Was she willing to do that? Hadn't she spent months striving to move on? What would be the point of throwing the towel in just because he wanted her as his lover for a week or two longer?

'I think,' she said gently, 'that it would be better…healthier…for us to leave things where they are, Curtis. Let's remember this as a wonderful one-off.' She kissed him lightly on the lips and began edging away from him. 'We're friends and, okay, it might be a little odd tomorrow, but after that…? Well, we'll still be great friends. I'll go on dates and stop burying myself in work and you… There's an ocean of gorgeous women waiting out there for you.' She smiled but her heart was clenched with pain. 'So I'm going to go back to my room now.'

The thought of having more of him was so tempting that she had to escape as fast as she possibly could or else risk being talked into something she knew she would end up regretting.

She slid her legs over the side of the bed and tried not to make a frantic, embarrassed dash to the pile of clothes on the ground.

The red dress no longer felt sexy. She was going to walk the plank of shame and thank goodness her room was next to his.

With a final glance at him, she said, amiably and calmly, 'Skiing tomorrow?' She paused. 'It's been really great, Curtis. I'll remember it for ever. I'll see you in the morning.'

CHAPTER SEVEN

AN UNEASY TRUCE. A sticking plaster over something that threatened to ooze out.

That was what it felt like to Jess.

Yes, she had left his bed, had got right back into that red dress and had scuttled back to her bedroom. And, yes, they had skied in the morning and chatted, but she was conscious of whole conversations lying unspoken beneath the surface of their banter and chat and laughter.

Was it just her who had felt the strain of trying to pretend that everything was as it had been *before*?

She'd laughed but made sure to keep her distance physically. She'd teased him while steering clear of all references to anything that could be a reminder of the fact that they'd slept together. She'd watched him and now her eyes were no longer innocent, no longer speculating. She knew what his body looked like and felt like and tasted like, and it had been hell keeping things natural while that imagery was playing in her head.

It had been a relief to hit British soil once again. As if mentally back behind his desk even before they arrived back at the airport, he had disconnected on the flight over, burying himself in whatever work he had missed during his time out in Courchevel.

She assumed that once his proposition had failed he had shrugged off her rejection with good humour and relegated the whole episode to the back of his mind. Easy come, easy go.

While *for her* that had been impossible.

A breather, she had decided. Once back, she would no longer have to be in his presence and so that spine-tingling, toe-curling, dark, forbidden excitement that had suffocated her would be gone.

They had parted company at the airport and she had firmly refused his offer of a driver to return her to Ely.

'Jess,' he had said, turning his fabulous green eyes on her for the first time since they had left the hotel, 'it's ridiculous for you to trudge all the way back to your house on public transport in this weather. If you don't want a driver, then I will get a taxi to take you back and if you don't want that, then I will have to insist on driving you back myself.'

She had taken the taxi. She had returned to her house and had spent the past two and a half weeks nursing all sorts of memories that had no place in her life. She had half-heartedly checked out a couple of guys on her dating app and rejected both. She had told herself that she just had a very bad case of breakup blues, which was something everyone went through but usually years earlier. She was a late bloomer but that didn't mean that she wouldn't recover, that she would remain trapped in a half-life of yearning for what she couldn't have while desperately trying to embrace what she didn't want.

She had immersed herself in work and repeatedly told herself that in six months' time she would chuckle at the torment she was currently feeling.

Except in six months' time…

Jess stared at the small stick with the pair of blue lines on it and felt a wave of nausea rise up inside her all over again.

Books to be marked sat untouched on her kitchen table. Although she had recognised two days ago that her normally perfectly reliable menstrual cycle had had a glitch, it had not seriously occurred to her that she might be pregnant. Not even when, two hours previously, she had gone to the local chemist to buy some toiletries and bought herself a pregnancy testing kit on the spur of the moment… *just in case*.

Now she was numb as she stared at the evidence of the price that could be paid for a few hours of stolen pleasure.

How? *How?* He had used protection, but then she thought back to his shock when he had found out that she was a virgin, the way he had fumbled, totally thrown by something that hadn't come close to registering as a possibility on his radar. Had he known that there had been a chance the contraception had failed? She vaguely remembered him muttering something before the moment was lost in the heady passion that had consumed both of them.

Experienced as he was with the opposite sex, he had clearly never been in the novel situation of ending up in bed with a virgin and, in that

once-in-a-lifetime moment of utter awkwardness, fate had seen fit to intervene.

And what happened now? she wondered miserably. Outside, steady freezing rain seemed to
mirror her panic-fuelled confusion and mind-
numbing fear.

Of course she would have to tell Curtis.
What choice did she have? On moral grounds
it would have been indefensible to keep that
sort of information to herself, and on practical
grounds it would have been impossible any-
way because she saw a great deal of his godfather. Hiding a pregnancy and a baby didn't
begin to be an option unless she turned her
back on her strongly held principles and fled
the area under cover of darkness. Like a thief
in the night.

Facing a very long evening with nothing to
do but think, Jess picked up her cell phone,
stared at it for a few minutes, her heart pounding like a jackhammer inside her, and dialled
his number. *Don't put off until tomorrow what
you can do today...*

It was a little after five in the evening which,
for Curtis, still left at least two, if not three,

hours ahead of him. Two or three work-fuelled hours before his driver returned him to his bigger-than-strictly-necessary house in one of the most expensive postcodes in London.

Life could have been better as far as he was concerned.

Work-wise? Great. More money being added to the coffers. Two enormous deals that would guarantee him as a major player in the cut-throat world of web development and complex data analysis.

But on a personal level…?

Two dates with two small hot blondes had failed to ignite his interest or, for that matter, put to rest way too many fantasies about a certain five-ten woman he had slept with *once* but who still managed to occupy his every waking moment.

For a 'moving on' type of guy, as he was, that did not sit well. Understatement. That sat very, very badly, especially when the blunt truth was that she had been the one to turf him out. Metaphorically.

Of course, as he had told himself over the past couple of weeks, she had been absolutely right. Parting company, when he thought about it, was key to making sure their friendship remained intact and that was the main thing. A bit of a dalliance, however much he had craved it at the time, would never be worth the risk of her getting hurt. Not that there had been the slightest chance of that because she had been very casual and very upbeat when she had turned him down. The last few hours they had spent together before heading back to London had been proof positive that theirs had been no more for her than an enjoyable and brief fling. Which worked for him too. Didn't it?

Every scrap of common sense he had deployed when he'd thought about the situation should have been enough for him to sally forth to pastures new without a backward glance, but unfortunately the opposite seemed to be the case. Was it because he connected with her on a level that went way beyond the physical? Was the bedrock of their friendship the thing that was making it so difficult for him to shut the door on that very brief interlude? However many bracing internal debates he had.

To further complicate everything, William

had read something somewhere and that was proving a thorny and unforeseen problem.

'Where did you hear that?' Curtis had asked two days ago when his godfather had casually mentioned that it was nice that the skiing holiday had resulted in the unexpected—in him and Jess 'becoming an item.'

It had taken half an hour of painstaking interrogation to discover that he had featured with Jess in the gossip pages of a weekly women's magazine of the type usually found lying on glass tables in hairdressing salons.

The picture was innocent enough, Curtis had discovered when he sprinted to the nearest newsagent to see what the fuss was all about. The text accompanying the picture, on the other hand, suggested all sorts of things that had given him an almighty headache. In a few short sentences, it implied that the most eligible bachelor in London had finally met his match and found the woman of his dreams. Would marriage follow…? it asked. It appeared that a 'little birdie' and 'good friend' had spilled the beans.

Curtis had no doubt as to the identity of the good friend and little birdie.

Caitlin had finally exited his life in a blaze of glory by making as much trouble for him as she could. Under normal circumstances, this would have amounted to no more than some awkward conversations with his friends but, against all odds, his godfather had read that article and now...

A headache.

'What were you doing with a women's glossy?' Curtis had been unable to stop himself from asking.

'Everybody needs some light relief, my boy!' William had answered testily. 'Happened to see it in a prominent place at the newsagents so got hold of it. Good to know what's happening out there with you young people! And good job I did! Don't suppose I would have heard a sausage about anything otherwise. Jess certainly didn't say a peep when she came round yesterday! Course, far be it from me to start interfering...asking questions...not my style at all.' And then he had added darkly, 'Nice you two have finally seen sense and decided to make a go of it, Curtis, but I'm warning you... Jess isn't one of those floozies you like to go out with, so I don't want you doing your usual.'

If not a catastrophe, then certainly a nuisance because, whilst he didn't care what other people thought of him, he *did* care what his godfather thought of him and so he had spent the past day toying with the realisation that he would have to talk to Jess and explain the situation before William decided to start asking her awkward questions about the relationship that never was.

So, sitting here now, unable to focus, Jess's name popping up on his cell phone felt propitious. For the first time since he'd got back to London his senses were on full alert and he felt *alive.*

He'd tried to contact her, left a couple of voicemails because she'd failed to pick up her phone and in return had received a brief text from her, claiming that she'd been frantically busy at work—telling him to have a good week.

So now...

Yes, he felt alive, senses zinging as he heard her voice. He pushed himself back and relaxed into his massive bespoke leather chair and stuck his feet on his desk, crossing them at the ankles.

'Jess!' For a few seconds, Curtis contemplated the satisfying notion that she might have been calling to tell him that she'd had second thoughts about continuing what they had started two and a half weeks ago.

Hard on the heels of that came the more realistic scenario, which was that William had had a chat with her, maybe shared his pleasure that she was now dating his godson, told her what a relief it was after all those *floozies*.

He abruptly swung his feet off the desk and sat up.

'How are you? Haven't heard from you in a while.'

'I've been busy.' At the other end of the line, Jess felt her breathing slow. Just hearing his voice, so deep and lazy and utterly sexy, caused a racing of her pulse and the faintness of pure excitement, and then she glanced at the stick in front of her and sobered up fast.

Her mind went blank for a few seconds and she surfaced to hear him saying something about his godfather.

'He's fine,' she interrupted. 'Curtis, I need to have a chat with you.'

'Isn't that what we're doing now?'

'I mean a *face-to-face* chat.'

Curtis smiled. William was fine. There had been no difficult conversation where she had had to try and figure out how, having firmly shut the door on their brief one-night stand, they were suddenly newsworthy and involved in a love-fest with wedding bells just round the corner.

But then why was she calling? Not just calling, but he knew her well and she was...*tense*.

Since when had Jess ever been tense with him? If she wasn't herself, then it was because she didn't know how to say what she wanted to say, and what else could that be other than the pleasing thought that she regretted her hasty rejection of his proposition that they continue what they'd started?

He'd spent the past couple of weeks with her inconveniently lodged in his head, and if it had been the same for her then it stood to reason that she had reached the very same conclusion he had.

'I could be with you in a couple of hours,' he said, promptly discarding the prospect of three more hours of work as he moved to rescue the grey cashmere jumper which he had tossed on the leather sofa by the window, along with his coat.

'There's no need to put yourself out, Curtis!'

'I'm already on my way.' He was. 'Where do you want to go for dinner?' He felt energised.

'Nowhere!'

'All the better,' he murmured smoothly. 'I get sick of eating out. Home cooking is so much better. Maybe I'll get William to give me a few lessons on the basics some time—he threatens to do it often enough. Would make an old man happy…' He was out of his office, barely glancing in the direction of all the worker bees still hard at it at their desks, including his extremely efficient middle-aged PA. He winked at her, mouthed that he would see her in the morning maybe…and then he was sprinting for the lift.

Jess realised that he'd hung up on her before she'd had time to fix another more timely date for them to meet. A date that would give her sufficient breathing space to get her thoughts in order and brace herself for a conversation she'd never dreamt she would ever have with him.

Instead, at a little after five-fifteen, she flew into action. Shower, change into jeans and a long-sleeve T-shirt…and then a mad dash to gather up all the ingredients she would need for an unwelcome dinner *à deux*. It wouldn't be the first time Curtis had had a meal at her house. That said, it was the first time she'd felt sick with nerves whilst preparing a meal. Pasta. Tomatoes and some mushrooms. Exactly what she had planned to have for herself, so she just had to double the quantity.

It felt as though ten minutes had passed when she heard the sharp buzz of her doorbell. She flew to the door and pulled it open and there he was. Six foot three of unfairly gorgeous masculine beauty. She breathed in sharply and stood aside to allow him to sweep past her.

He brought the cold in with him, along with a bottle of wine, which he handed to her before divesting himself of his coat and making his way into her kitchen, as comfortable in his surroundings as though he lived there.

Her heart was thumping so hard she felt faint. He'd always had that peculiar ability to somehow consume all the oxygen, until she felt she couldn't breathe, but never was she more conscious of that than now.

'There was no need for you to rush over here, Curtis.'

'Why are you looking so tense? Glass of wine?'

'Er…no, thank you.'

'Let's go relax in the sitting room.' He moved towards the door, having helped himself to some wine from the bottle he brought and glanced over his shoulder at her, grinning. 'Where have you been, Jess? Tried calling you a couple of times. Sure you won't join me in a glass? No one likes to drink alone.'

'I've been busy,' she muttered, already feeling helplessly in thrall to him and incapable of thinking straight. 'And no, thanks.'

He frowned. 'What's the point of an injection of cash if they're still slave-driving you into more fundraising?'

'I haven't been fundraising. I've been catching up on work and preparing the kids for their next batch of exams.' He'd perched on the deep, comfortable sofa and now looked at her with a veiled expression, his head tilted to one side. Expecting what? she wondered. Expecting her to have relented on his proposal, she guessed, because he was just too tempting to resist. Why else would he have rushed all the way up here?

To forestall a conversation that would lead nowhere, she cleared her throat and perched on the chair facing him.

She rested her hands on her knees and thought about that tiny beating heart inside her. It had not crossed her mind even for a second that she might not keep this baby and now she felt a flutter of excitement, against all odds.

He didn't say anything. He was quite still, his green eyes penetrating.

'Curtis...about what happened when we were away together a few weeks ago...'

He relaxed and smiled. 'Yes?' he prompted softly.

'You remember when we...when...?'

'When we made love?' His smile broadened and there was dark, lazy appreciation in his eyes that sent a wave of longing rushing through her with toxic potency. 'Unforgettable,' he added huskily.

'I had never…done it before…'

'I haven't forgotten.' His voice was unsteady in recollection. 'Believe me, it's imprinted in my memory banks with the force of a red-hot branding iron. Come sit by me, Jess…'

'You fumbled.'

'Come again?'

'It was a shock. You were caught on the back foot for a few seconds. You…fumbled…'

'Maybe I did. We all have our moments.'

'Curtis, the protection you used wasn't as foolproof as maybe you thought it was.'

Jess watched as comprehension filtered through the self-assurance that was so much part and parcel of his personality. The easy, sexy smile faded, he frowned, then the frown cleared and the colour drained from his face.

'What are you saying?'

Jess thought that he knew very well what she was saying but he just didn't want to believe it.

He'd had that situation with Caitlin. He'd found himself cornered into a marriage proposal he hadn't wanted because, at the end of the day, he wasn't into commitment. What must he be thinking now? Was he terrified that he was about to find himself in another corner?

'Curtis, I'm pregnant. I took the test this morning.' She shifted her eyes from his shocked, ashen face. 'I know you didn't come here expecting this, but you had to know. I don't... I'm not expecting anything from you,' she rushed on clumsily. 'I realise that this must be your worst nightmare come true, but I'm not Caitlin.' She laughed nervously and slid her eyes back to his face. No change there. He still looked as though he'd spotted that the sky was falling down and there was no shelter in sight.

'You're not Caitlin...'

'I don't want anything from you.' She slapped her hands on her thighs and began standing. 'So, now that I've told you...er...if you still want to stay for some pasta...or you might just want to go away and think about... er...things... No rush—you can call me when you're ready.'

She began walking away, but she didn't make it to the door. He was there in front of her, barring the exit, and the colour had returned to his face.

'*Go away*?' he grated in outraged disbelief. '*No rush*? Call you when I'm ready? Maybe next week…? Next month…? Next year…? Oh, I'm going to be staying for some pasta, Jess. I'm not going anywhere any time soon, until we've dealt with this situation!'

After the most stressful few hours she had ever had, Jess suddenly saw red. She leaned aggressively towards him, eyes narrowed.

'*Dealt with this situation*? How do you pro-pose to do that, Curtis? There's nothing to deal with. It's happening and we just have to ac-cept that!'

'I need another drink. Something less polite than a glass of wine.' He raked his fingers through his hair and stared at her.

How could this be happening? How had this *happened*? He knew she was right. He *had* fumbled. At the time he'd registered that pro-tection had not gone according to plan but then the thought had been lost and had not resur-faced. And now here they were and, although the bomb had been dropped, he still couldn't believe that life as he knew it was about to implode.

But she must be as shocked as he was. Her colour was hectic and her deep blue eyes, always so soft and laughing, were filled with apprehension, anger at him and uncertainty.

Pain twisted, and shame that he had allowed himself to lose control, to hurt her with badly constructed phrases, poured through him.

'Let's go into the kitchen, Jess,' he said rather more quietly, 'and talk. Let's not forget the most important thing. We're friends. Not enemies.'

For the first time Jess felt some of her nerves dissipate because he was right. They weren't enemies. Far from it.

He spent a few minutes helping her prepare the food, which was a first, and they did that in silence.

When they were sitting in front of their bowls of pasta he looked at her seriously.

'First of all,' he said heavily, 'you're not Caitlin and, whether or not you expect anything from me, I intend to be fully involved.' He dug into his pasta, twirled the spaghetti round his fork and ate a mouthful, watching her in silence.

'Yes, and I wouldn't dream of getting in the way of you doing that.' She had no appetite, but she was aware that this was not the time to start toying with her food. For the next nine months she would be thinking about the well-being and health of the child she was carrying and again, despite the circumstances, she felt that punch of pure excitement at the thought of becoming a mum. 'I'm happy for us to informally arrange…visiting rights, even though it's early days yet.'

'Visiting rights…?'

He made it sound as though those two words were ones he'd never heard in his life before. Jess figured he was probably right on that score. He might have known what they meant but certainly not insofar as they pertained to him.

'I don't think we need to involve lawyers. I will never fight you when it comes to something like that.' She paused. 'And I guess,' she continued awkwardly, 'you'll probably want to financially contribute…?'

'Does that question really demand an answer?' But there was still that dazed look on his face, which made her hesitate for some reason.

'I guess not,' she conceded. 'But, whatever you decide to contribute,' she told him firmly, 'I want you to know that it will never be for *me*. It'll be for the baby.'

'So I buy the clothes and the…the baby food and the nappies and leave you to carry on teaching and trying to make ends meet?'

Jess looked around her and grimaced. Through the eyes of a billionaire, even one who happened to be her friend, was this little house ever going to make the grade? His pockets were deep enough for him to treat her to one of the most expensive ski resorts on the planet. How was he going to feel about their child coming home to a house where there was hardly enough room to swing a cat?

But the follow-on from that line of thinking was one she knew she would find impossible to accept.

A kept woman, given whatever she wanted financially because she was his child's mother. She enjoyed her independence—*loved* it—but how much joy would she have bringing in her

204 CONSEQUENCES OF THEIR WEDDING CHARADE

own modest salary when she knew that it was irrelevant?

And if she refused, what would he do next?

Yes, they were friends, but the ground would shift irrevocably underneath their friendship with a child in the equation.

Where she lived, the lack of space, the cramped neighbourhood—all of that would now enter the realms of his concern. Would he think about claiming custody of their child? If he genuinely felt that he could provide a better life for a child because of his vast financial base, then wouldn't he just go for it? Whilst still telling her what good friends they were?

Jess knew that the racing of her mind wasn't going to get her anywhere, but the first drips of cold fear trickled through her as scenario upon scenario formed in her head.

'Money isn't everything, Curtis,' she said weakly. 'Think of all the rich people you know who aren't happy.'

'William knows about us.' Curtis abruptly changed the subject and she gaped at him for a few seconds, her mind still occupied with raging worst case scenarios.

'What are you talking about?'

'We were papped at the wedding. The picture was innocuous enough. The accompanying text less so. I had to wrench the hows and wherefores out of him, but the bottom line is that all the innuendo in the very brief few sentences under that picture imply a serious relationship between the two of us.'

'But did you set him straight?' Jess gasped.

'No.'

'Why not? When did you have this conversation with him? He never mentioned a word to me about anything!'

'He didn't want to appear nosy. The reason I didn't put him straight was because, as you pointed out, William's mental health has not been great since he said goodbye to active life at the university. Also...'

'Also?'

Curtis flushed and pushed his bowl to the side so that he could relax into the chair whilst continuing to look at her with brooding intensity. 'Also, he seems to think that I'm the sort of guy to take advantage of you for my own nefarious purposes, only to dispose of you when I get bored.'

'Ahh...'

'Define *ahh...*'

'I suppose...' for the first time during their fraught conversation she was diverted enough to smile as years of friendship kicked in '...you *do* come with some form in that department, Curtis.'

He grimaced and returned her smile. 'My track record doesn't do me justice.' He raised both hands in mock surrender as her eyebrows shot up. 'Okay, I can see why he assumed what he did, but Jess, it *does* leave us in a bit of a quandary in light of this new development.'

'Why?' She stuck her chin out at a mutinous angle. 'William wasn't born yesterday, Curtis. He knows that not all relationships end in marriage, that sometimes that's not possible.'

'Sometimes,' Curtis told her quietly, 'the head doesn't always win the argument.'

'What are you trying to say?' Jess demanded helplessly.

'Marry me, Jess. I suppose that's what I'm trying to say.'

She gaped at him in open incredulity. '*Marry* you?'

She wondered whether she'd missed a vital link or a sentence somewhere, but then she remembered that he had proposed once before to a woman he hadn't wanted to be with for the sake of the child she had purported to be carrying for him. He was a decent guy. It was why she…had always liked and admired him. More than that. But decency didn't win when it came to a lifetime together. Love held all the trump cards in that respect and, as much as Curtis liked her and respected her and had fun with her, and had even made love with her, he didn't *love* her.

He was prepared to do the right thing but, face it, she thought with painful honesty, he was a guy with a very healthy libido and a penchant for 'moving on' when it came to relationships. Once the enthusiasm for doing the decent thing had worn off and once William had been satisfied in assuming that his godson had sticking power when it came to her, Jess, then what would happen next?

Discreet affairs?

He would break her heart. She loved him. She'd loved him for ever and she expected she always would. It was an admission she had managed to bury in her subconscious but now she took it out, aired it, faced up to it and accepted it with a certain amount of dull resignation.

Marry him and she would be left picking up the pieces and she would never be able to glue them back together again. Wasn't that why she had walked away from the temptation to carry on what they'd had in Courchevel? Hadn't she known, even then, that she had to protect herself?

'Of course I'm not going to *marry* you, Curtis! I wouldn't hurt your godfather for all the tea in China, but I also won't sacrifice my entire life to a loveless marriage. I deserve better than that. We *both* do.'

He looked at her in silence for so long that she began to fidget.

'I'm not prepared to be a part-time parent,' he told her.

'What do you mean?'

'I mean I'll do whatever it takes to ensure a child of mine gets the very best that life has to offer, and that includes a full-time father.'

This was the steel hand in the velvet glove, Jess thought numbly. A guy didn't climb the greasy pole to get to the very top by being Mr Nice Guy. He might be fair and generous and witty, and often surprisingly thoughtful, but he could also be tough when he needed to be. Now, it seemed, was one of those times.

'Are you *threatening* me, Curtis?'

'I'm asking you to think long and hard about my proposition and to put yourself at the back of the queue, as I am prepared to do. A child needs two parents whenever possible, Jess. That's something I would fight tooth and nail to achieve. It's more important than any other consideration.'

CHAPTER EIGHT

'TOMORROW...' HE SAID, vaulting upright. 'We can talk tomorrow. You tell me that I need to go away and think about what you've lobbed into my life? Well, *you* need to have some time to think about the only solution I would find acceptable in this situation. I'm going to head to William's, and I intend to stay there until we've come to an agreement on this.'

'No!' Jess sprang to her feet and, rather as he had earlier, she swerved round him to bar his exit. Hands on her hips and feet squarely planted on the ground, she glared at him.

'Come again?'

'No way, Curtis Hamilton, do you get to tell me that you're prepared to fight me over this because you happen to believe in "the sanctity of family life"! One minute you're waxing lyrical that relationships are a waste of time, and then in the next breath you're telling me that we need to get married for the sake of a baby!'

He flushed and raked his fingers through his hair. '*Relationships* aren't a waste of time,' he muttered. '*Love* is the pointless component.'

'So you're prepared to walk down the aisle with a woman even though you don't love her.'

'If there is a child involved, then yes. I am.'

'Why, Curtis?' There was genuine curiosity in her voice. This guy was the epitome of a forward-thinking male, one who was tuned in to women in the workplace, who made sure that there was no discrimination between the sexes when it came to pay and promotions. Three years previously, Jess could remember reading an article about his massive company being a leading light in the war against all forms of discrimination.

So how was it that he could be so stubbornly *traditional* when it came to something like this?

It wasn't even as though she wanted to bar access to his child. She was prepared to bend over backwards to accommodate him!

'I…' He stared at her, at her puzzled expression. 'I wouldn't mind a coffee,' he muttered, shifting uncomfortably under her direct gaze.

'Okay.' She stepped aside.

The atmosphere had shifted, and she couldn't really even work out *how*, but it had. Her heart began to race. There was a peculiar vulnerability she couldn't *see* but could somehow *sense*.

She walked ahead of him to the kitchen and felt his eyes on her as she bustled about making them both a mug of coffee. She didn't have to ask how he took his because she knew. No milk and a heaped teaspoon of sugar. She'd teased him often enough that sugar in coffee was unnecessary.

'You have to see it from my point of view, Curtis,' she told him quietly, positioning herself opposite him at the small table and cradling the warm mug between her hands before taking a sip. 'I just don't get it. I don't want to fight you on this. Not at all. And from where I'm sitting, any child we have will have us both. We just won't be living together. We won't be sacrificing our chance to find true love and happiness with someone else because the unexpected has happened. You should be *relieved* that I'm not trying to force your hand!'

'I… Before William rescued me…' Curtis stared into the depths of the abyss and took the plunge. Confession. He'd never considered it good for the soul. His past was his and his alone but now he felt an unexpected rush of relief that he was going to do what he had never been tempted to do in his life before. Share. 'Before William rescued me... I was in care.' His eyes met hers. He was already resenting any show of pity but there was none in her clear gaze. She simply tilted her head to one side, her expression urging him to continue. He found that that was something he wanted to do.

'I have no idea who my father is. He'd fled the scene, presumably, before I was born. Maybe he took flight at the prospect of an unwanted kid. At any rate, my mother...my mother was clever and beautiful. She was also a drug addict, something she got into when she left university. William knew her when she was a student. He was her tutor and he took a paternal interest in her because she was, I expect, something of a lost cause despite her brains. From the little I know about my mother's background, she had been left to her own devices from day one and by the time she hit fourteen she was pretty much doing her own thing. It's surprising that she ever made it to university at all but, like I said, she was bright. I suppose, in the end, background ended up winning the war over brains. To cut a long story short, William was transferred to Australia shortly after I was born, shortly after my mother decided to get me christened. Maybe she had a premonition that her lousy parenting would require someone to one day step up to the plate. Who knows? At any rate, she overdosed when I was still young and I was put into foster care. And there I remained for over two years until, through sheer good fortune, William found out about me and rescued me.'

'I'm sorry, Curtis.' Jess hesitated, so tempted to delve deeper yet knowing he would shut down if she did. 'You want your own child to have what you feel you never had yourself.'

'It trumps everything.'

'He or she can have that without us getting married. As you've said, we're friends. Not enemies.'

'Which is what makes marriage all the more appealing. No delusions. Solid grounding in a mutual desire to do what's best for the child.'

Jess realised with consternation that that was the very reason why she couldn't marry him. Where, for Curtis, friendship would be the glue between them, creating harmony in the joint desire to do what might be best for a child that hadn't asked to be conceived, for her friendship where she craved love would be a daily torment. It would be a constant reminder that she wanted more from him and, more dangerously, because she knew herself, a constant battle against hope.

'I can't marry you, Curtis. We have to find another way forward and I hope that way won't involve you trying to fight me for custody of our child.'

'I wouldn't do that.' He stood up. His expression was blank. 'William will have to be told.'

'Yes.' She had drawn her line in the sand and her heart was breaking in two. What he had told her had made her want to weep but she knew that she had to stand firm or else end up hopelessly lost.

William, though, was going to be an almighty problem. He didn't want to hurt his godfather, for powerful reasons she was only now fully understanding, and nor did she.

She knew that William would assume his godson had somehow taken advantage of her and had ended up with a mess on his hands, and even if she denied anything of the sort he would still secretly judge Curtis, who would be found wanting for ever.

It would be heartbreaking.

Curtis had inadvertently told her that William had *rescued* him and that was a very telling word. Could she live with herself if that relationship was somehow changed for ever for the worse?

She could live with herself if *their* friendship changed. It almost certainly would now that she had turned down his proposal. But for William to blame Curtis for what had happened…? That would be a great deal harder to stomach.

He began heading towards the door and she reached out and stayed him with her hand on his arm and felt him stiffen under her touch.

Already their friendship was changing.

'I get it.'

'What do you get, Jess?' His mouth twisted. 'That my semi-tragic background is responsible for me making unreasonable decisions when it comes to the fate of a baby?'

'No!' But she reddened.

'You want your freedom to find true love and I can't stop you. The conversation has been had and, as you've said, it's time to move onto another solution to handling this situation. I said I would do anything within my power to give any child of mine what they deserve. That doesn't mean trying to fight you for custody.'

His voice was cool, accepting and practical, and it cut a jagged path through her heart.

'William...' She maintained eye contact but removed her hand from his arm.

'It is what it is.'

'I can understand,' she said softly, 'why it means so much that his opinion of you isn't... doesn't...'

'Like I said,' Curtis grated, 'it is what it is.'

'Believe it or not, it would break my heart if I thought I'd done anything at all to change his opinion of you,' Jess said. 'So here's *my* proposal.'

'I'm listening.'

'Tomorrow we'll tell him...um...about the situation, but I'm prepared to paper over the fact that we're not cementing a relationship by rushing down the aisle.'

'Explain, Jess.'

'We can pretend just for a while that this isn't what it actually is…a one-night stand with unexpected consequences.' She paused but his expression was unreadable. 'I know if it tapers off in due course, he will more easily accept that we had fun but that as lifelong partners it wasn't meant to be. He won't…think that you're the bad guy in this…he won't think that you used me. Which, of course, you didn't.'

She watched as he lowered his eyes, shielding his expression.

As sacrifices went, this was a big deal for her because she would much rather have dealt with things in a businesslike fashion, which might have protected her battered heart, but his story…his heart-wrenching account of a childhood she had never suspected…

We all had our Achilles heel. If he was hers, then William was his.

To pretend a relationship for a short while would be worth it if it saved William's opinion of his godson. He adored Curtis and she wouldn't want to see that jeopardised.

'Appreciated,' Curtis said curtly. For a couple of seconds he seemed to be on the verge of adding to that, but instead he inclined his head in a mocking salute. 'Tomorrow,' he told her brusquely. 'Do you want to come to the house or would you rather I swing by to fetch you?'

'I'll make my own way there.'

She felt a shiver of apprehension at a future stretching out in front of her, weaving its obscure way to a place she didn't know and hadn't banked on.

It was nearly midnight by the time she finally curled up in bed and it was a long time before she actually managed to fall asleep.

William was chatting in the background. The kitchen was aromatic. Smells wafting of a full English lunch with all the trimmings. Lounging on the kitchen chair, one eye on the time because Jess would be arriving at midday, Curtis sipped his wine and half listened to what his godfather was saying. There was no need to give undivided attention because he knew the gist of the conversation and the reason he knew was because William had been stuck in the same groove ever since breakfast.

He swerved between utter joy at the prospect of his godson and Jess finally getting where he had hoped they'd get for a long time and dark warning words about him not taking advantage of one of the nicest girls on the planet.

Curtis had more or less been obliged to respond in a series of non-committal murmurs that neither encouraged nor discouraged but he was immeasurably glad that Jess had come up with the idea of maintaining a pretence of sorts for a short while.

She'd read the situation perfectly and he knew that she'd been swayed by what he'd told her, the confession he'd never thought would ever leave his lips.

A confession he did not regret having made, astonishingly.

Had all that hurt he'd carried around like a dead weight for all his life been somehow diffused the minute he'd confided in her? He certainly felt weightless now. In the telling, he had shed the demons that had plagued him, although, and he knew this with gut certainty, she was absolutely the only one he would ever have told.

Trust.

He trusted her.

He trusted her—he enjoyed her company—and, in more ways than one, they were *good* for one another. He couldn't understand why those things weren't enough to sway her, to make her see what he wanted her to see!

He'd told her about his past. He could never love. His heart was cold but that didn't mean that all of him was buried under ice. Affection, surely, ranked as high as love. Strip away the high-minded, exalted, overrated emotional insecurity of love and what you found was that the relationships that lasted could fall back on good old affection.

So far was she from Caitlin, with her manipulative drive to get him, whatever the means, that he knew he should be overjoyed, but he wished there was some way he could get to Jess, get her to see his point of view, get her to marry him for the sake of their unborn child.

He was lost in introspection when the doorbell rang, and he leapt to go to the door even as William was putting lids on pans and wiping his hands on his apron.

'Stay here,' Curtis told him. He smiled but

tension was snaking a path through him. 'That lamb isn't going to roast itself without some TLC...'

'Son, are you okay? You've been very quiet this morning.'

Caught on the back foot, Curtis shuffled and raked his fingers through his hair and glanced at his godfather. 'There's something...'

'Something *what*?' William's shrewd blue eyes were suddenly sharp and very focused.

'Something Jess and I need to talk to you about...'

'Don't tell me anything you think I might not want to hear,' William countered sharply.

Another piercing ring of the doorbell saved him from any further elaboration and on his way to open the door Curtis decided that coming clean about the pregnancy was the best way forward. What would be the point of a great elephant in the room, sitting between them at the dining table for the duration of lunch?

'Jess.' He swung open the door and drew in a sharp breath. In the shock of the unexpected the day before, his libido had taken a back seat. Now it came back in a hot rush as he stared at her, dressed in her usual thick padded coat with a yellow and black woollen hat pulled over her head and some faded jeans and sensible wellies visible under the coat. The least sexy outfit on the planet and yet the heat that surged in him could have melted steel. Involuntarily, his eyes zoomed to her belly before he quickly averted them.

'You look amazed,' she returned, but her smile was tentative. 'Did you think I might have bailed?'

'I've told William that we have something to say to him.'

'Already?' Her eyes widened in sudden alarm and she chewed her lip anxiously.

'It's going to have to be done, so why not immediately?'

'I guess...'

'You're scared?'

'I don't like lying.'

'This was your idea,' he pointed out, then added with grudging honesty, 'not that I'm not grateful.' He stood aside so that she could brush past him but they remained in the hallway, facing one another. 'He's...on a high with this news of our sudden romance.' He grimaced. 'Admitting the truth at this juncture would have been a little…'

'Terrifying?'

'Dramatic word.' But he smiled, amused, and raised his eyebrows. 'Hence I am very grateful you decided to…indulge in a very gentle white lie that will smooth the path for all of us.'

She followed him towards the kitchen. The cottage was cosy and comfortable. No sharp edges or stark colours or empty spaces. Nothing jarringly modern. She loved it. This was the first time she'd felt nervous being here but she sidestepped the feeling. Curtis was right. It was better to say what had to be said and get it out of the way. It was also a good thing that they would be indulging in this harmless white lie because William would have been devastated to think that she was going to have a baby with his godson without any attempt at a relationship to cement them. Who could blame him? He was an old-fashioned man who had grown more and more jaded and impatient with Curtis's choices when it came to the opposite sex.

'So,' he greeted them both from the doorway of the kitchen, arms folded, his eyes sharp, 'what's this big thing the pair of you want to talk to me about?'

Jess smiled and kissed him fondly on the cheek. 'That's a very gruff way to greet me, William. A girl could be offended. What's on the menu today, chef?' She sniffed the air and noted how he relaxed, which then made her realise just how keyed-up he was about Curtis, braced, no doubt, for another speech about his godson not wanting to relinquish his casual approach to relationships, but this time with *her* in the starring role of discarded victim.

'Lamb. Your favourite. And don't think I'm going to fall for you trying to distract me, young lady. Now, tell me what it is you have to say.'

But he was moving off, nodding at the table, because dining was always casual, in the kitchen, at the eight-seater wooden table by the French windows that led into the neatly manicured back garden.

'Would I do that?' Jess teased, exchanging a quick glance with Curtis. Her face betrayed none of her nerves as they all sat, as Curtis looked at her, as they said, speaking briefly over one another—

'We're having a baby...'

Remove all the signposts and how was anyone supposed to know where the next misplaced step might put them?

We're having a baby.

Those four words had removed the signposts. That was what kept running through Jess's head as, two days later, she and Curtis sat in one of the old-fashioned tea rooms in Ely, looking at one another over a pot of tea and a plate of scones at three-thirty in the afternoon.

Outside, wintry skies were leaden with the promise of snow. In here, though, it was warm enough for them both to have shed outer layers and she had to try very hard to ignore his intense masculine appeal, as she had been for the past day and a half, during which time, at William's insistence, she and Curtis had been spending a crazy amount of their free time together.

'You kids might go back a ways,' he had announced with satisfaction over the perfect lamb lunch, 'but that doesn't mean a court-ship isn't a good thing and, correct me if I'm wrong, but have you two ever courted one another? You are having a baby together and I may be an old-fashioned fool but I feel it's important you make the most of the free time you have together before a demanding little one starts calling the shots! Not that this old fool won't be more than happy to babysit!'

So here they were, having tea and scones in the middle of a freezing cold Friday afternoon. She should have been at home, prepping her syllabus for the following week, taking advantage of the fact that it was a class-free afternoon, thanks to an induction day for new students. He should have been in London, working. She vaguely thought that they should have been communicating by email or WhatsApp, whereby she would not be forced to try and sublimate responses that ambushed all her efforts at self-control the minute she was in his company.

The evening before, William had cooked them both a fabulous dinner and then promptly abandoned them so that he could go to the pub, where he'd planned on meeting a couple of old friends. *'What friends?'* His answer had been vague. *'Why the urgency?'* Answer also vague.

'When do you have your first scan? Have you been to the doctor? Booked anything?'

'Huh?' Startled out of her brief reverie and surprised because the weather and the possibility of snow had been the last topic on the agenda, Jess looked at Curtis with wide-eyed surprise.

Their eyes tangled and she blushed.

'Not for ages and no, I haven't been to the doctor.'

'Shouldn't you register?' He looked at her narrowly and she reddened even more.

'I've been busy.'

'When you go, I want to be there.'

'Do you?'

'What did you expect?'

'Well… I know we're pretending to be involved for William's benefit, but he's not ear-wigging here, Curtis, so there's no need to… er…show an interest at this…um…early stage.'

'I'm not,' he told her abruptly. 'I want to be there every step of the way.'

A vision of intimacy swamped her as she imagined him standing next to her while they looked at a scan in a darkened room with her swollen belly exposed.

She changed the subject quickly, to clear the image from her head. 'How long do you think we're going to have to pretend that we're... serious about one another for William's benefit?'

Curtis tensed. Could she make it any clearer just how little she enjoyed the situation?

Of course, neither of them had thought that William would have stuck his oar in to the extent of insisting they spend quality time together instead of just talking to one another on the phone.

Curtis thought that her hair would curl if she knew the full extent of his godfather's belief that they were madly in love, that it was just a question of time before they tied the knot— because why on earth would they want their baby to be born out of wedlock?—and that plans should be made about where they intended to live.

He had done his best to avoid being pinned down but the prospect of disentangling themselves from the fabrication they had concocted was beginning to look a lot less simple than either of them had originally thought.

That should have worried him. This enforced mini break should have worried him. Since when did he spend time lazing around when there were deals to be done? The fact that it didn't worry him was even more disturbing.

Clearly, though, he was on his own when it came to guiltily enjoying this predicament. He'd seen a different side to her in Courchevel. In bite-sized pieces over the years, he hadn't really appreciated just how smart and funny and empathetic she was. It had been a journey of discovery and so what if he was enjoying the fact that the journey hadn't ended? It made sense because they were going to co-parent, whether he wanted more or not, and so he needed to spend this time with her, to further see the woman who was bearing his child.

'He's very much invested in this,' he said, taking his third scone. 'Time, of course, will allow us to demonstrate that we won't be spending the rest of our lives in blissful perpetuity. How much time? How long is a piece of string?'

* * *

Jess frowned. 'I don't know how long the piece of string is, Curtis, but maybe we should try and measure it.'

She was aghast at the prospect of having to deal with her wayward emotions for an indefinite period of time. She saw him and she wanted more, and she hated herself for wanting more. He'd dropped all mention of marriage and she could only think that he was relieved not to have been pushed into anything. Maybe he'd had time to think what a nightmare it would have turned out to be—married to a woman he didn't love, a woman who should have stayed firmly put in the *friend* category.

'At any rate, surely he can't expect you to wash your hands of your work commitments in London?' She tilted her head to one side. 'You must be distraught at having to hang around here when you hadn't planned to.'

'Could your language be any more colourful? Distraught?'

Jess ignored the interruption. She hated the way that sexy drawl could make her whole body tighten with sexual excitement. There was a slight smile tugging the corners of his mouth and she ignored that as well but she could still feel a slow burn inside her.

'But I have an idea that I think might work,' she slowly suggested, frowning when he raised his eyebrows in a vaguely sceptical question.

'Can't wait to hear.'

'You head back to London tomorrow, first thing. Maybe even later this evening. You then stay away for a while due to pressure of work—time issues...meetings abroad...money to be made, deals to be done et cetera. While you're away, I'll lay the foundations for a relationship that couldn't possibly survive because of your long absences. Of course, I'll make sure he knows that we will always remain the best of friends, but that we're just not suited for anything more than that.'

'Due to the fact that I'm never around.'

'Well,' she pointed out defensively, 'you *do* devote most of your time to work'

'Hmm. So...to recap,' Curtis mused pensively, cool green eyes boring into her until she had to struggle not to squirm, 'you generously engineer the demise of our short-lived relationship on the grounds that I'm a complete bastard who can't be bothered to stick around for his own flesh and blood because making more and more money is vastly more important.'

'I didn't say that there weren't elements that couldn't be fine-tuned,' she snapped. 'It's just an idea, Curtis, because we both know that, sooner rather than later, we're going to have to come clean and the later we leave it, I'm now beginning to see, the harder it's going to be.'

'I'm not being the fall guy in this little scheme, Jess. I'm the one who was willing to get married and do the right thing. *You* were the one who was so invested in the business of finding Mr Right that you're willing to walk away from marriage. So when it comes to wriggling out of this arrangement you can forget it if you imagine I'm going to be nailed to the wall as the man who won't step up to the plate and do the honourable thing.'

Hot and bothered, Jess glared at him.

Why was he being so difficult? She knew. His background demanded he provided for his child what his own feckless mother had failed to provide for him and she was stricken by a sudden attack of guilt, but then many children who didn't have irresponsible parents managed to do very well in a situation where their parents no longer lived together. Essentially, she argued with herself, their own child would have a very different experience of growing up than he had had.

Of course, she could see that he might have been a bit taken aback by the rough outline of her idea, but surely he was as keen as she was to keep this charade as short as possible.

Did he still imagine that she would rush into marrying him after she'd said her piece?

Maybe he did. It wasn't as though he knew just how deep her feelings for him ran, just how catastrophic it would be for her to sign up to being his wife, to being with him every minute of every day, knowing that what she felt for him would never be returned.

She was hit by a sudden wave of pure despair as all-engulfing as a tidal wave and she felt tears prick the back of her eyes.

And, just like that, he reached out and held her hand, his eyes filled with concern.

'Don't stress,' he said roughly.

'But I *do* stress,' she whispered.

'You're scared.' He paused and squeezed her

hand, a gesture of such tender support that her heart clenched. 'You don't want the uncertainty of our situation hanging over your head indefinitely, like the Sword of Damocles...'

She shook her head, not trusting herself to speak.

Curtis sighed and rubbed his eyes before looking at her gravely. 'I'll make sure...the way is suitably paved.' His mouth twisted into a smile tinged with sadness. 'As it seems I can't persuade him down any other route. He's arranged a small dinner tonight, asking one of his friends over. After that? Don't worry. It'll be...sorted.'

CHAPTER NINE

THE DINNER WAS at six-thirty or, as William would have said, 'six-thirty for seven', being a stickler to the traditional rules of etiquette. With family, there would be casual drinks before dinner at the kitchen table, but he always took great pride in the formalities of 'proper dining' when he had guests, so drinks would be taken in his front room and dinner would be in the dining room, even though there would be just the one guest.

She hoped the evening wouldn't be too awkward and was already feeling a twinge of sorrow for his disappointment when it had to be broken to him that, whilst he would still be a grandparent, he would not have a daughter-in-law in *her*.

How did Curtis plan to take care of this situation? He had told her that it would be sorted. How?

Would he have said something to William

already? Or would he do as she had suggested, which seemed a sensible route towards demonstrating through action rather than words that they were a couple who were not temperamentally suited for any kind of long-term relationship, whether there was a child in the mix or not.

The promised snow had turned into a flurry of flakes falling steadily by the time she hopped on her bike for the twenty-minute cycle-ride to William's cottage.

In jeans and her trainers and two layers of jumpers and with her woolly hat pulled low over her head, she was still freezing by the time she finally arrived at the sprawling cottage in its acre of beautifully manicured grounds.

Cold and fifteen minutes late.

She was tugging off her fingerless gloves when Curtis pulled open the door before she had time to press the bell for a second time.

'You're late,' were his first words as he fell back to let her past him, closing the heavy front door on the swirl of snowflakes.

Jess blinked and stared at him. Would he *always* take her breath away like this?

A plain black long-sleeved, semi-fitted T-shirt emphasised the width of his shoulders. He had shoved up the sleeves and her eyes were drawn to the curl of golden-brown hair around the metallic watch strap. His jeans were faded black and he wore a pair of loafers. He looked exactly what he was—a sophisticated, uber sexy billionaire who could snap his fingers and have any woman he wanted.

It seemed just a tiny bit disingenuous that William could actually find it credible that his godson might fall for her.

'I cycled.' She pulled off the woolly hat, which was wet from falling snow, and shook out her hair. 'Took longer than I'd anticipated. The roads are treacherous.'

'Why the heck didn't you drive, Jess?'

'My battery's low.'

He raked his fingers through his hair with evident frustration. 'This isn't going to do.'

'What are you talking about?'

Still divesting herself of layers of clothing because the cottage was beautifully warm, she was barely looking at him as she spoke.

'Taking chances, Jess! Look at the weather!

It's snowing. Of course it's not only going to take longer to get here, but the roads are going to be worse than treacherous! You could have gone flying over the handlebars of that bike! Have you forgotten that you're pregnant?'

'Of course I haven't forgotten, Curtis!' She damped down the pleasurable warmth from his protective, possessive outburst and reminded herself that this was all about the precious cargo she was now carrying.

'You should have called me. I would have driven over to fetch you.'

'I'm perfectly fine to look after myself,' Jess told him. 'I'm pregnant, not ill. I made sure to be very careful on the bike.'

'It's time you had a new car. I'll sort that out.'

'You'll do nothing of the sort!'

'Since when does anyone fight over the gift of a new car? I'm rich. You're having my baby. Stop being so sensitive over small things.'

Jess sighed but accepted the offer. Because he had a very valid point and it was something she would just have to get used to. She wanted her freedom? Then with that would come his inevitable desire to make sure she wanted for nothing, because for her to need anything implied that his child would, likewise, be in need.

Her independence was about to be eroded and she didn't think that the erosion was going to be a subtle advance.

'Okay, Curtis, but please, if you insist, then I will choose what I think is appropriate.'

'Appropriate for whom?' But he had relaxed and was looking at her with amusement. 'You're unique, do you know that?'

Jess blushed, at a loss for what to say, but before she could say anything at all he continued, far more seriously, 'I was distracted.' He placed his hand on her arm and turned her to look at him.

The harried expression she had glimpsed when he had opened the door for her was back and she looked at him with alarm.

'Distracted?'

'You arriving on a bike…the snow…the fact that you could have had an accident, cycling like a maniac in weather like this.'

'I wasn't cycling like a maniac!'

'William's mystery guest…'

'What about her? Him? Who is it?'

'I don't think you're going to like who will be joining us for dinner.'

'You're scaring me. Why won't—?'

At which point a beaming William emerged into the hall, and behind him was a short, rotund man with a goatee beard. One of William's friends. Probably a professor from the university. He kept in touch with a handful and was wont to display his culinary expertise for them every so often.

Why is this a cause for concern? That was the thought that sprang to mind as she moved forward, smiling.

'Jess!' William's beam got brighter as he approached her with his hands outstretched, dapper in a pair of navy trousers, a formal long-sleeved shirt and a snazzy royal blue bow tie. 'You look delightful. That colour suits you, my dear.'

'Grey?' She laughed out loud. 'Thank you, William. I'll bear that in mind when I next go clothes-shopping.'

Behind her, Curtis's presence made the hairs on her neck stand on end. She was uber conscious of his presence and uber conscious of her own weakness whenever he was around.

'Don't believe you've met my friend, have you?'

Jess peered past him to the chap behind, who was of similar age to William and also looking rather delighted. She sensed that news of her pregnancy might have been imparted. Was that what Curtis had been worried about? It was certainly a worry he would have to get used to because there was no way her pregnancy was going to remain a secret for very long and definitely not in William's circle of friends.

'No...'

'Allow me to introduce Raymond! Raymond Dale. He's the local vicar and—exciting news—he's agreed to marry you!'

'What...? Sorry...?'

'Don't stand around there in the hall, you two. It's cold out here! Come through to the sitting room. I've prepared some delightful morsels.'

For Jess, where the past few weeks had whipped by with the speed of sound, time now seemed to stand completely still.

The evening progressed in a haze of appalled confusion as they were ushered by a benevolent William into the sitting room, where drinks were being served.

Raymond was as charming as they came and after fifteen minutes he settled into a jovial but thoughtful line of questioning about what they expected from marriage.

Jess suspected that this had been well planned in advance by William who, at this point, removed himself from proceedings to 'see about supper'—which was going to be a surprise, he told her, but she must rest assured some of her favourite things would be served, including homemade tiramisu for pudding.

'Sit, sit...' William encouraged, before his opportune departure from the room. He then proceeded to usher her and Curtis into the small two-seater sofa by the fireplace, allowing his friend to angle his chair so that he was facing them both.

She felt the press of Curtis's thigh against hers, a distraction she could do without.

Even more distracting was when he took her hand in his, without looking at her, so that he could link fingers with her.

With no room to shuffle out of reach, she pinned a glazed smile to her face and let her hand go limp, even though the racing of her pulse was quite enough to remind her of the devastating effect that small gesture was having on her nervous system.

What on earth was he playing at? she wondered.

Of course, he might not want to alert the local vicar and his godfather's friend that their relationship was not what it appeared to be, but surely he shouldn't be actively *encouraging* the illusion by holding hands. Wouldn't it have been more appropriate for him to have taken up a position on another chair? One of the ones in the furthest reaches of the sitting room.

Her jaw ached from the artificial smile she kept plastered on her face as she listened to Raymond's kind words of advice to the couple due to be married.

'Money,' he intoned, carefully sipping from his modest glass of sherry, 'really is the root of many an evil. It's a cliché, my children, but one I would urge you to both consider as you contemplate your way forward together.'

Jess nodded. Next to her Curtis was more forthcoming, holding forth on how much he agreed with the sentiment, having seen many a person come a cropper in their haste to make it to the top, often taking down their loved ones with them.

He squeezed her hand and she smiled faintly. She could feel beads of perspiration breaking out. She didn't want to be discussing a marriage that was never going to happen, and not just because it was unfair to propagate the illusion to someone who was sincerely trying to give them good advice.

She didn't want to discuss this because in her head it raised so many tantalising visions of what could have been if only...

In this situation there was no room for *if only*, so she did her utmost to let the litany of wise advice sweep past her, keeping a low profile, barely aware of how Curtis was responding. Just aware that he *was* responding.

Dinner couldn't have come soon enough.

The food was spectacular and, thankfully, the conversation moved on to less disconcerting waters.

She allowed herself to relax. A bit.

She tried several times to catch Curtis's eye, but his attention was focused on his god-father and Raymond and, sitting as she was, right next to him, there was a limit to what she could do to engage a surreptitious response from him.

And in the meantime...

How her mind travelled down all those for-bidden paths that talk of marriage had opened up in her head.

She had so many memories of her parents, of how deeply in love they had been, enjoy-ing the time they'd spent together as a family.

Had such happiness on the home front made her ill equipped for the realities of life and all its complexities?

Shy as a teenager because of her height and the fact that she had developed earlier than most of her classmates, she had been too re-served to throw herself into the ups and downs of teenage dating games. Instead, she had en-joyed her books, her sport, her skiing when-ever she could.

Maybe if she had had her heart broken a few times she would have been more protected against the business of daydreams and unrealistic expectations.

Except what was so wrong in having expectations in life? It was just unfortunate that her expectations had sent her racing towards a brick wall.

As the evening wound down to its conclusion, Jess could only reflect on the irony that she and Curtis were two people so conditioned by their backgrounds that never in a million years would they have found a fit together.

Where her own sheltered and cosy life had prepared her to follow a predictable course of love and marriage and children, his fractured one had sent him hurtling down a different route.

It was her misfortune that she had tumbled into love with him and now faced the prospect of trying to piece her life together without him, even though she would never be able to fully walk away because of the glue that now held them together.

'You've been very quiet this evening, my dear.'

She surfaced and blinked at William, who was looking at her with paternal concern, and her heart wrenched at the disappointment he would be facing when she and Curtis broke the news to him that they wouldn't be getting married after all.

Raymond was beginning to stand, patting his stomach with satisfaction and complimenting William on the quality of the food.

Jess glanced through the window to see that the snow was falling ever harder, teetering towards blizzard rather than angry flurries.

They all began heading towards the door. Raymond had driven and waved aside William's suggestion that he stay the night and give the snow time to blow itself out. He had a sturdy four-wheel drive, he asserted, and he had every confidence that the Big Guy up there would make sure he was in full functioning order so that he could marry his close friend's godson to his partner.

Jess smiled weakly, very much aware of Curtis's hand resting lightly on the small of her back as they clustered in the hallway, reaching for coats and winding down the conversation.

'So...' Raymond paused, winked at William and then smiled at them all. 'I'm ready to marry you two just as soon as you want.

Of course, there'll be a few bits and pieces to sort out—i's dotted and t's crossed and all the rest—but I have slots in my upcoming diary and I don't have to tell you that I will do my utmost to accommodate the ceremony whenever suits you both!'

'I think these children would want sooner rather than later.' William beamed at them both. 'With a baby on the way, why waste time?'

'Why indeed?' Curtis murmured, and Jess gaped sideways at him, but no one was looking in her direction because all eyes were on Raymond, who was doing all but fetching his personal calendar from his coat pocket.

'There's no rush,' she interjected weakly.

'Two weeks, Raymond? A fortnight? Give you young things plenty of time to start sorting out the details about where you're going to live. Of course, far be it from me to say anything about the folly of bringing up a baby in central London, however big the mansion might be, but then that's just the opinion of an old fool...'

Those words were ringing in her ears when, less than five minutes after Raymond had gone, William offered his godson's services to return her to her house.

'Although, my dear, you're more than welcome to stay here.' He shot them both a crafty look from under bushy brows and grinned. 'Curtis, your room's made and I dare say a double bed would do for the both of you…?'

She promptly opted for the ride home and waited in dithering low-level panic as William bustled off upstairs, waving down her offer to help tidy the kitchen, whilst Curtis disappeared to store her bike in the garage.

No sooner was the car door shut on them and the engine started than she spun to him and said, restraining herself from shouting, '*What* is going on, Curtis?'

Fists clenched on her lap, she peered at his averted profile as he calmly manoeuvred the four-wheel drive down towards the lane at the bottom of the front garden.

She realised that whilst she had been panicking for most of the evening as she'd felt herself sucked deeper and deeper into a trap not of her making, *he* had remained firmly in control, giving nothing away, as charming as he always was. Charming and doing absolutely nothing to avert the impending storm on the horizon.

Underneath the charm, if only she could read what he was thinking, but she couldn't. He was a marvel when it came to concealing just exactly what he didn't want to reveal and right at this moment she was at a loss to decipher his thoughts. She assumed that surely he must be thinking as she was, alarmed at the fact that they had somehow found themselves manoeuvred into a situation they hadn't anticipated.

'It seems,' he drawled, concentrating on the road, taking it slowly as the snow gathered in swirls around the car, spraying against the windscreen wipers, 'that William is in something of a rush to get the formalities out of the way.'

'Is that *all* you have to say on the subject?' Jess all but cried in utter frustration.

'I can't focus on driving if you talk.'

She snorted, glowering, but fell into impatient silence as he carefully wended his way to her house, easing the car to a stop directly in front and killing the engine.

'Before you launch into a full-scale post-mortem of this evening,' he began, unbuckling his seat belt, 'let's go into the house. I need warming up with some coffee.'

There was no need to look at her to know that the unfolding of the evening had horrified her.

Her silence had been telling. He had almost *felt* the stiffness behind her responses and had done his best to paper over it.

In truth, he had been as startled as she had been by the presence of the local vicar. The revelation that his godfather and his friend had concocted a hastened schedule towards a wedding had shocked him, but he had kept his reaction firmly under wraps.

Anything else would have been inappropriate.

And really, how surprised should he have been by both developments? Not very. It had become clear over the past few days that his godfather's disapproval of his private life ran deeper than Curtis had ever imagined.

That hurt. Of course he knew that William was fashioned along more traditional lines. Of course he knew that his godfather didn't care for the revolving door approach to relationships that Curtis favoured, but in the past there had been no overt discussions on the topic.

However, things had changed dramatically on that front.

In short order, Curtis had been made aware of just how much William despaired of his history of brief liaisons. There had been relief when he had broken off his engagement with Caitlin because, as William had finally told him in no uncertain terms, wherever that match had been made, it had definitely *not* been in heaven. But since then…? Curtis's return to his bad old ways had been a source of deep concern and disappointment.

That had been the very word William had used and never in his life had Curtis felt so wretchedly *lacking*.

So now that he and Jess were together, with a baby on the way, William couldn't have been happier. Threaded into that happiness, though, he had managed to bluntly inform his godson that any return to his 'love 'em and leave 'em' ways would be unacceptable.

It shouldn't have come as a shock that William wasn't going to tolerate a loose timetable when it came to tying the knot and he had therefore taken matters into his own hands and hurried things along at a pace that had left Curtis spinning.

The fact that he *wanted* to marry the mother of his unborn child was also a source of intense frustration.

Throughout the course of the evening, he had slanted surreptitious looks at Jess and he knew her well enough to establish that she was no closer to accepting his marriage proposal now, in the face of the rushed schedule William had chosen to spring on them, than she had been when he had first suggested it.

She didn't want to marry him. She liked him, she had fun with him, and they were sexually more than compatible, but she *still* didn't want to end up with him permanently by her side. Underneath the liking and the fun and the good sex, it was clear that he just didn't quite cut it.

Now, as they stepped into her small house and he began removing his coat, he realised that that *hurt*.

Why? Why did that hurt? When he had always taken such care to protect himself from anyone having the power to inflict any sort of emotional pain on him. He suddenly felt a wave of nausea wash over him, temporarily dulling his ability to think straight, then his head cleared and he wondered whether it was just a case of his ego having taken a blow.

Made sense, didn't it?

But he still felt rattled as they headed straight for her tiny kitchen.

'Well?' she demanded, hands on hips, as he took his time settling into one of the kitchen chairs that always felt way too tiny for him.

Her deep navy-blue eyes were narrowed accusingly on him and Curtis shifted uneasily, for once in his life on the defensive.

'Are we going to get into an argument about this?'

'Yes, that's a definite possibility, Curtis!'

'Why don't you sit down instead of towering over me like an avenging angel?'

'How on earth could you let William believe that we're going to be married *within a fortnight*?'

'If memory serves me, we were both present when that announcement was made.' But for once his agile mind was refusing to do what it usually did so well, manoeuvre through the problems and cut straight to the chase.

She had managed to break through his defences.

That was the sobering thought at the back of his mind. It wasn't about his ego being a little bruised. He was hurting because…because… because she had managed to break through his defences and leave him open and vulnerable.

When had that happened? Before they'd slept together. Before he had become blatantly aware of her physical attraction. With blinding clarity, he recognised that she had made stealthy strides deep into the very core of him and, bit by bit, she had stolen his heart.

She might not want him as a long-term proposition because she was looking for someone more suitable, and he knew that there was no way he could force her hand and neither would he want to.

Wasn't the depth of love measured by the painful ability to walk away if that was what the person you loved wanted?

Because he loved this woman. He loved her in all her moods. He was addicted to her laughter and her generous spirit and her sense of humour, which was so like his. He loved this woman because she got him in ways no one else in the world did, and that included his godfather.

If he had to take the hit with his godfather, if he had to sink in his estimation in order to be the person who let go the object of his love for her own good, because that was what she wanted, then so be it.

He felt he could no longer look at her and he scowled at the effort of averting his hungry gaze.

'What are we going to do?'

Jess could feel the walls closing in around her. It was one thing to promote a small white lie with an indefinite timeline. It was quite another when the small white lie grew sharp teeth and the timeline shrank from indefinite to just round the corner.

When she thought about being propelled into living with Curtis, a ring on her finger, trapped with someone who didn't love her and who, inevitably, would grow to resent her oppressive presence in his life, she broke out in a cold sweat.

'How can you be so…so *calm*?' she demanded shrilly. 'Did you have any idea of what was going to happen this evening? Did William say anything to you? Why would he want us to get married *in two weeks*?'

'You're horrified,' Curtis said flatly.

'Of course I'm horrified! Aren't you?'

'It was my idea for us to get married so I'm hardly going to be quite as horrified as you seem to be.'

'I can't marry someone just for the sake of a child, Curtis. We've been through all this already! That sort of union would destroy both of us in the end.' She had a vivid image of him sneaking out in the dead of night for an illicit rendezvous with a small, adoring blonde so that he could have hot sex with someone more to his liking and complain about the shrew he had been obliged to wed because of his godfather.

It jarred that she knew he wasn't that sort of person, the sort to have clandestine affairs, but who knew how anyone might react given certain circumstances?

Married and with a broken heart that got a

little more broken day by day was not a future she wanted for herself.

If she could never have a clean break because of the fact that they shared a child, then surely as clean a break as possible would be the best option?

She missed his dark flush and the tightening of his lips as she continued to visualise a future that had been brought to within touching distance by William.

She blinked to find him rising to his feet, turning away from her, and there was such finality in that movement that she yearned to reach out and stop him.

'You understand where I'm coming from, don't you?' she questioned anxiously, following him out of the kitchen and then hovering indecisively as he began putting on his coat.

'Of course I do,' Curtis said coolly. 'You've made that crystal-clear.'

'It's important we remain friends,' she pointed out with a hint of panic in her voice. She could feel his cold withdrawal like a physical blow. 'We've always been friends. We need to continue being friends because of... well, now that there's a baby on the way. Aside from the business of...of *love*, we both know that it would be hopeless being married.' She laughed but the laugh emerged as a cross between a croak and a sob. He was looking at her in silence now, head tilted to one side, his expression remote.

'Whereas...whereas we can both step back from the brink and deal with this in a civilised and *amicable* manner! Whatever you'd like, I'm happy to go along with.' Her previous mental block when it came to accepting his largesse now seemed petty and childish. 'I totally get it that you might think my house is a bit on the small side...' She waited for him to lighten up, to pick up the bait she had thrown and tease her about the dimensions of her one up, one down, but he remained coolly, disconcertingly silent, which propelled her further into heated, rambling speech. 'So I'll understand if you want to house us both somewhere a little bigger...' Still that shuttered expression and glacial silence. 'I won't fight you over that. I know you think that the best thing for us to do is to get married, but if you really thought about it you'd agree that in the end we would hate one another!'

'And on that note,' Curtis told her, turning away, his voice husky, 'I think I'll leave.' He slung on his coat, turned back to look at her. 'If it would make things easier for you, I am happy to arrange the details through a lawyer.'

'No! Why would you want to do that, Curtis? We're not enemies, we're friends. Isn't that what you told me?'

'Sometimes clarity is needed in certain situations, Jess. I don't want you to feel uncomfortable having to deal with me when you'd rather I took...a step backwards.'

'No!' She wanted to reach out and clutch his sleeve but instead she folded her arms and stared at him, not too certain how it was that the ground had shifted so dramatically under her feet when all she'd been trying to do was find out what the heck was going on and how they could rescue the situation. 'I don't want lawyers involved!'

'Because that's not what friends do? Especially friends who have ended up in bed with one another?'

She went bright red and was momentarily lost for words and into that silence he said, in a flat, calm voice, 'Your bike? I will ensure that it's returned to you first thing in the morning. And as to my godfather—you needn't worry that you're going to find yourself in any awkward situations, having to carry on with a pretence you no longer wish to be a part of. Tomorrow morning I'll sit William down and explain the situation to him.'

'You will?' She blanched at the thought of how disappointed his godfather was going to be, swept from the euphoria of hastening their marriage vows to having to accept that there would be no exchange of vows after all, and all in the space of twenty-four hours, without any time to adjust, as she had hoped might be the case when she'd suggested this charade.

'If you choose to contact him to explain the situation, then fine. If not, also fine.' He spun round on his heel and headed for the door while she disconsolately padded in his wake, shaken to the core by the grim finality of every word that had crossed his lips.

'Of course,' he continued, hand on the door knob, ready to leave, 'I will be in touch often and we will naturally have to meet up to discuss details of how we move forward if there is to be no involvement with lawyers, but rest assured I will not invade your space in any way, shape or form.' He rested an almost gentle gaze on her as he opened the door, letting in a rush of freezing cold and the spray of snow. 'Your personal happiness, Jess? There is no way I would ever think to get in the way of you achieving it…when all is said and done, it's what you deserve.'

CHAPTER TEN

JESS CAME TO a stop outside William's house and dismounted her bike.

The snow of the week before had given way to ice, blue skies and penetrating cold.

Not great conditions in which to hop on a bike and cycle, but her car had finally given up and she was waiting for a replacement, courtesy of Curtis, who had been in touch with her at least once a day since they had parted company nearly ten days previously.

She had mentioned that she was cycling to school because of her lack of alternative transport and, sure enough, he had immediately insisted on remedying the situation by replacing her dud car with something that actually, in his own words, had 'an engine built this side of the Boer War'.

She hadn't quibbled. Ever since their last conversation he had been the perfect gentleman.

Of course, it was impossible to gauge how

he felt exactly, because it was very different being face to face with someone as opposed to hearing a disembodied voice or reading a text message but, true to his word, he had explained the situation to his godfather.

'How…how did he take it?' she had asked anxiously and he had set her mind at rest with his answer.

'He accepted it. Don't we all. Accept the things we can't change.'

Like a coward, Jess had left a few days for the dust to settle with William and she had refrained from probing when she'd spoken to Curtis.

Something about their relationship had shifted and she couldn't quite put her finger on it.

He had retreated.

It felt as though their relationship had moved through stages, from the comfort of friendship to the angst of infatuation, from the desperate urge to break free to the magnetic pull of something too strong, from the passion of being lovers to the sadness of accepting a love that would never be reciprocated.

But where she was now felt the worst.

She was in the most intimate place two people could reach, with his baby inside her, and yet she had never felt more separated from him.

For better or worse, he had been a constant in her life for as long as she could remember but now, despite his support, she could feel that constant slipping away.

He was doing all the right things because he was a decent guy.

He was concerned about her, keen to make life as easy as possible for her, asked her whether she was eating okay and feeling okay and doing okay.

They had begun to tentatively discuss housing arrangements which, he had told her, would take time and so should be sorted as soon as possible, because he would rather their baby be born in the place where they intended to put down firm roots so that there was no inconvenient upheaval with an infant.

'Where will you be based?' she had asked and had been fobbed off with a something-and-nothing answer.

'Perhaps I might think of investing in something closer to William,' he had hinted. *'Within*

easy commuting distance of where you are so that visiting can be maintained on as regular a basis as possible...'

The implication was that he was keen to ensure her happiness and, to that end, would be amenable to whatever she wanted.

It was all going so much better than she could ever have hoped, she told herself with bracing optimism as she slanted her bike against the side wall and buzzed the doorbell.

She'd laid down her rules and regulations, had point blank refused to marry for reasons she knew he privately accepted when you dug beneath his adherence to do the right thing, and he had backed off just as she had hoped.

In the end, they had both found a meeting place where they could now communicate like two perfectly civilised adults with a passionately shared interest in the child they had conceived together.

She felt William would be pleased with that outcome, although the second he opened the door her heart dived and her nerves kicked in and she gave him a watery smile as he ushered her inside.

'No need to be nervous.' He bustled her into

the kitchen and cut to the chase before she had time to start on the pleasantries. 'I was an old fool to think the pair of you might actually get married!'

Thrown in at the deep end, Jess let him make her a cup of tea and fuss over her health, all the while bemoaning his short-sightedness in expecting more than would be forthcoming.

There were no accusations directed at *her*, which she interpreted as indicating that all accusations were mentally directed at Curtis, and her heart went out to Curtis, ached at the thought of him losing standing in the eyes of the one person in the world he loved and re-spected.

Which was why, when there was a breather in the conversation, she said tentatively, 'You shouldn't blame Curtis for anything.'

'Blame that godson of mine?' William huffed, settling into the chair facing her and fussing with his teacup. 'Wouldn't dream of it! My fault. Expected too much. Forgot that the world we live in now isn't quite the same as the world I lived in back in the day!'

'He did suggest that we get married,' Jess

countered quietly. 'It was important to him because of what he went through as a child.'

William stilled and looked at her with a suddenly guarded expression. 'Explain, dear child.'

'You know—' Jess looked down to gaze at her fingertips '—being in foster care for those two years, living life as a young child who never got the security and stability kids need because his mother...failed in that respect. Those things made him propose marriage as a way of making sure his own child had the security he lacked, and it's only because I objected that those wedding bells won't be ringing.' She raised her eyes to look at him and, for once, she could read absolutely nothing on a face that was normally so expressive. She hesitated but, having taken the plunge, her only way now was to carry on until she felt her feet on solid ground again.

'I wanted more than duty. I wanted love because, without love, duty would become a very empty vessel. I couldn't bear the thought of the two of us ending up squabbling and unhappy in a loveless marriage, which would have been a disaster for the child.'

'Curtis told you about his past?'

'He did.'

'And you didn't think that was reason enough to wed? There is also the fact that you are in love with him—'

'He would never love me back!' Jess cried, then flushed as the significance of her outburst hit home. 'I mean… What I mean…'

'My dear, there's no need for either of us to dwell further on this.' He waved down her anguished attempt to explain what she meant, and it was fair to say that he seemed remarkably more upbeat now, insisting she stay for some dinner. 'You wouldn't want an old man to eat by himself, would you? Besides, you need feeding up!'

Relieved at the change in atmosphere, Jess would have accepted any invitation in pursuit of further pouring oil over troubled waters. It wasn't yet five and marking schoolwork would have to wait. It wasn't as though she had anything else lined up expect a scintillating evening nursing her thoughts.

'I just have a quick phone call to make.'

She nodded and helped herself to another cup of tea as he bustled out of the kitchen to his telephone in the sitting room. It had been silly to have been so nervous about this meeting. Of course he would understand! He might be the only person left in the county who still insisted on using a landline, but that didn't mean he was a dinosaur when it came to all things modern.

Curtis was on his way back to London from a meeting not a million miles away from Ely when he got the call on his phone and picked up on Bluetooth.

William.

His heart sank. He had spoken to his godfather several times since he had broken the news about the wedding that wasn't to be. Each time he had ended the conversation with the depressing realisation that nothing was going to be the same again between them, or if they *were* to return to what they'd been then it would take a long time.

He shuddered when he recalled the horror of telling William that he and Jess, much as they were going to remain the closest of friends and united as they were in wanting the best for the child they had created, would not be getting married.

A joint decision, he had said, and one they had both agreed on. They would never stop being the best of buddies, he had insisted, and through gritted teeth had muttered something about wishing her every happiness with someone she loved.

He had contemplated heading to Ely after his meeting but, with the ground still so rocky and uncertain with his godfather, he had chosen to postpone a physical meeting until the following week, which would have allowed some of the dust to settle.

It would also have allowed him time to psych himself up to seeing Jess. He had spoken to her on the phone and messaged her, but seeing her in the flesh?

Bittersweet.

He picked up the call and went into something of a panic when the first words William uttered were, 'Son, you need to head up here as soon as you can.'

Jess was chopping some tomatoes when the doorbell buzzed. William, who seemed distracted, had spent the past forty-five minutes flapping around the kitchen, alternately explaining the roux he was making whilst finding fault with her chopping skills.

One of his favourite daily radio shows was playing in the background.

He dropped everything at the sound of the doorbell. Wrapped up in her thoughts, Jess was vaguely aware of the sound of voices in the hallway but only when the kitchen door was pushed open did she turn around to see what the fuss was all about.

The last person she expected to see was Curtis and how her heart leapt at the sight of him, gloriously handsome in a charcoal-grey suit and a crisp white shirt. He had dispensed with the jacket and if he'd been wearing a tie it was no longer in evidence.

He looked *fatigued.*

He stopped abruptly in the doorway and now they stared at one another, oblivious to William's presence to the side. Indeed, Jess only remembered that he was there at all when he scuttled into position between them and announced with ringing confidence, 'You two need your heads banged together and I've decided that I am the one to do it. I'm going out for a couple of hours, and when I come back I want to find that the pair of you have come to your senses. You love one another and it's time to stop making a dog's dinner of the situation!' With which, he bustled back to the door, only pausing to toss over his shoulder, 'And the carrots, dear girl, still need to be julienned!'

'Jess...'

Curtis was the first to break the silence, giving her time to try and gather her scattered thoughts, but she couldn't, not when he was standing there in front of her, reminding her just how potent his impact was and making a mockery of her pretence that being away from him might have dented the force of her love. It hadn't.

'What are you doing here?'

'William called an hour ago. Said I had to get here. I was on my way back to London... I thought something was wrong, thought he might have had some kind of turn.'

'Curtis...'

'I'm glad I'm here, Jess. We need to talk. We should talk. I need to talk.'

'Haven't we already done that?' But her ears were ringing with William's incendiary remarks. How could he expose her love like that? And to have misinterpreted what his godson felt about her!

'About what your godfather said...' Her laugh was falsetto high and tapered off into conspicuous throat-clearing.

'He's right.'

'Sorry?'

'Let's go into the sitting room, Jess.'

'I have no idea why William thought that I... that...' Her cheeks were stinging and she knew that she was bright red. Pillarbox-red was not the colour of someone innocent of accusations.

She trailed behind him, mind frantically working to find a way out of William's parting shot that would enable her to emerge with some semblance of dignity.

Once sitting, she leaned forward, hands planted on her knees, every ounce of her attention pinned to his beautiful face.

He looked more than fatigued. He looked exhausted.

'You work too hard,' she said shortly and then realised that what should have sounded

like concern had instead morphed into ac-
cusation. She decided that that wasn't a bad
thing because he needed to realise that having
a child on the scene would require an end to
the twenty-four-seven work regime, and also
attack seemed the best form of defence, at least
right at this moment in time, when her heart
was flip-flopping dangerously inside her.

He looked at her with such searing intensity
and uncharacteristic confusion that she went
even further into defensive mode.

'You're going to have to do something about
that,' she said crisply. 'If you want to have a
good, solid relationship with your child. Also,'
she added, 'it's just bad for you, working all
the hours God made.'

'I haven't been working,' Curtis responded
quietly.

'What have you been doing? You look shattered. No, don't tell me…' she said, painfully
aware that there was one other thing guaranteed to tire a man out and it involved handling
statistics of a completely different kind.

'I've been thinking about you.'

Now it was Jess's turn to look confused. She
opened her mouth but nothing emerged.

He was leaning towards her, their postures mirroring one another's, and she sat on her hands to stop herself from reaching out to touch what was forbidden.

'Jess, I asked you to marry me...' He inhaled sharply, waiting for her to interject, but her vocal cords were still in a state of disarray. 'I put it to you as something of a business deal, something that would guarantee the sort of stability that I never had. Of course you're right. A marriage is no guarantee of stability and two people sharing the same goal can provide as stable an environment for a child even though they might not live with one another.'

'That's right!' She found her voice but there was not the ring of confidence in her assertation as she had hoped.

'I made a mistake.' He paused and took a deep breath. Jess had never seen him this hesitant before and it was disconcerting because he was a man who lived life in charge of the world around him. 'I should have been honest with you but, in fairness, that would have meant me being honest with myself and that was something I had no idea how to do.'

'I don't understand what you're trying to tell me, Curtis.'

'I have never bought into the whole love thing, Jess. You know that. I've always been upfront with you…with every single woman I've ever had a relationship with. No love meant no pain and, as far as I was concerned, that was a blessing. I'd had enough pain as a child to last a lifetime. Why would I court any more by letting my emotions take control? But you…you crept under my defences and I can't even exactly tell you when that happened. I just know that we slept together and something inside me was liberated, even though I wasn't aware of it at the time. And far less aware of the consequences.' He looked at her, his green eyes solemn, and tentatively reached out, encouraged when she, equally tentatively, touched his fingers with hers.

'I would never want to hurt you, Jess. I was fully prepared to walk away and give you the freedom you tell me you want, freedom to find the right guy for you, but I would never be able to live with myself if I hadn't first told you how I feel about you.'

'How you feel about me…' Jess's brain was

not quite keeping pace with what she was hearing.

'You mean everything to me, Jess. I think back and realise that, in many ways, you always have. You've been my foundation and I never realised just how strong the building blocks of what I felt for you were until, perhaps, we slept together. It was...' he smiled '...would magical be over the top?'

'No.' For the first time she smiled with pure happiness and joy. 'It would be just...the perfect word.' She finally allowed herself to touch his face and it felt good to stroke his cheek and to have him capture her hand between his so that he could place a tender kiss in her palm.

'I've been in love with you for such a long time, Curtis. It was only when you got engaged to Caitlin that I realised I was in danger of becoming one of those sad old spinsters who spend their lives pining for a guy who doesn't want them and eventually filling the void with... I don't know...cats or stuffed toys or stupid online dating...'

'Now she tells me.'

'I never dreamt that we would ever end up in bed together and when we did...it blew my mind. But I knew just where it would lead, which was why I knew that I had to walk away. And then I found out that I was pregnant...'

'And you turned me down even though you were crazy about me.'

'Who could *not* be crazy about a guy as modest as you, Curtis?' She laughed but then sobered to look at him seriously. 'I ached when you told me about your past. I finally understood why you were the person you were, such a giant when it comes to being thoughtful and fair and generous-minded, yet so fiercely guarded with your emotions. I could understand why you would want to marry for the sake of your child, but it would have destroyed me being married to someone I adored, knowing that they could never return my love. And we were friends, as you kept reminding me.' She grimaced. 'The word *friend* had never been one I didn't want to hear from you! But of course we *were* friends, and I knew that if we didn't marry we would always do what was best for the child we had conceived together, and at least then I might have been able to construct some sort of life for myself. Eventually.'

'But now,' he drawled, smiling, 'as things stand…will you, Jess Carr, my friend, lover and the woman I can't live without, be my wife?'

'I don't think you could stop me.'

EPILOGUE

ALICE ELIZABETH HAMILTON was born two days after her due date and entered the world without fuss, to be placed in the arms of her blissful parents who, in time-honoured tradition, had been married for five months.

The ceremony had been a quiet affair in the local church and, with only the smallest of bumps heralding the arrival of their daughter several months into the future, they had had their honeymoon in Courchevel, although this time the weather was somewhat different and there was no skiing on the agenda.

They had stayed a handful of days and then had completed the honeymoon at Lake Como, staying at one of the most beautiful hotels overlooking the flat blue of the lake.

And then they had begun the hunt for somewhere suitably large enough for a family.

Jess had dismissed anything too grand. 'Who needs eight bedrooms?' she had asked wryly when they had looked around the first house, which had been sourced by the relocation company Curtis had decided to use, so that excess traipsing around unsuitable properties could be filtered out.

After a month they had found the perfect cottage just half an hour away from William and from which Curtis would commute to London as and when he needed to. He'd refused to consider any situation that might involve him splitting his time between London and the suburbs.

For Jess, the fairy tale she'd never thought could happen had happened, and only after Alice was born did she finally manage to wean herself away from having to pinch herself every so often just to make sure that the life she was living wasn't just a dream from which she would wake up.

Dreams, she had discovered, really could come true.

* * * * *

LET'S TALK
Romance

For exclusive extracts, competitions
and special offers, find us online:

📘 facebook.com/millsandboon

📷 @millsandboonuk

🐦 @millsandboon

Or get in touch on 0844 844 1351*

For all the latest titles coming soon,
visit millsandboon.co.uk/nextmonth

Want even more
ROMANCE?

Join our bookclub today!

**Visit millsandbook.co.uk/Bookclub
and save on brand new books.**

MILLS & BOON